I0743464

BIZARRE EVENTS

EVE DELANGE

Printed in the United States of America.

ISBN   978-1-951913-23-6   (Paperback)
ISBN   978-1-951913-24-3   (Digital)

Lettra Press books may be ordered through booksellers or by contacting:

Lettra Press LLC
30 N Gould St. Suite 4753
Sheridan, WY 82801, USA
3035861431 | info@lettrapress.com
www.lettrapress.com

Other Books By Eve DeLange

Betrayed
Teen Sex Slave

This book is dedicated to

My Daughter, Remee Perillo

Who is the Strongest

Kindest and most Compassionate

Person I Know!

Chapter One

FBI SPECIAL AGENT RAGETTI just didn't want to get out of bed. It was his first day to go back to work since his honeymoon and his beautiful bride was lying right by his side.

Victoria poked him and said, "It's your first day back to work, you really shouldn't be late."

"I know, I know" Ragetti answered. But his heart wasn't in it. But when his wife slipped out of bed and went to the kitchen, he really had no excuse to stay in bed. By the time Ragetti entered the kitchen he had showered, dressed and looking, if not feeling, more like an agent.

"Why is the first day after vacation so hard?"

Victoria leaned down and gave him a quick kiss and told him it's just a normal reaction for everyone. "But once you get to work, you'll be eager to jump right in and see what's going to be your first assignment."

Ragetti scowled and looked at Victoria. "Why do you get to stay home and I have to go to work?"

"Come on, Sweetheart, don't do this again. I've already explained that with vacation ending on the last day of the month, our shift change starts on the first of each month; so they didn't want me to come back to work until tomorrow."

He sat down and tried to act happy that Victoria had made him breakfast. "Thank you for making breakfast, honey. You know this isn't necessary when you're not on the day shift, I love it; but I don't want you to change your schedule from what you've always done."

"We'll just settle in and see how it works out – now get going before you're late."

Ragetti backed out the driveway and looking up at his house still had a hard time believing this mansion was really his house. Would an FBI Agent fit into the neighborhood? I guess he would know soon enough, now that they would be living here full time. His old bachelor pad had been sold already and I think Victoria said she and Patty had an offer on their old house. By the time his mind had drifted through all that information, he was pulling up in front of the station. He saw that his partner, Smitty, was already here and so was Victoria's sister, Patty, who served as their researcher. He felt a little guilty at being the last one to work, it had been the first day back to work for all of them; so he should not have been late.

Cheers greeted him as he came through the door. Patty had his coffee poured and they both looked at him and pointed to the clock. It looked especially strange for Ragetti to be the last one to check into work, as he was usually there before anyone else.

Ragetti ignored the teasing and went over to give Patty a hug, even though he had just seen her at the house the night before. Then he turned to his partner and gave him a hug. "How was your vacation? Did you, Susan and the boys do anything special while you were off?"

Agent Smitty gave him a smile and said, "Well, I'm sure I didn't have as much fun as you did, after all you were on your honeymoon whereas I'm an old married guy with kids."

"Yeah, yeah, you have it really tough Smitty, and I feel for you, I really do."

Patty spoke up and asked, "What are we supposed to do now? Do we just sit here drinking coffee or how do we learn what our next case is?"

Smitty looked at her with pity, "Are you such a workaholic that you can't even enjoy having a half hour to just sit and relax drinking coffee? You two definitely make a good team. Knowing you I would guess that all our records are right up to date, and filed away. It has been so different since you took over this office. In fact, I'm quite sure that we are the only two agents who are lucky enough to have a researcher working under them. And on the subject of vacations I've never seen a more beautiful tan than yours. Did you lay out sun tanning your entire vacation?"

"I did spend a great deal of time swimming and tanning and I'm glad you like how it looks on me." Patty replied.

Smitty grinned at her and said, "You could have stayed right in that new house of yours and done that, but you probably paid big money to go to some fabulous spa."

Patty was about to give him a bad time but just at that moment Deputy Director Brown walked through the door. All they could do was stare at him; in all the years Ragetti had worked for the FBI he had never seen Brown go to an agent, he always called the agent and said "come to my office."

Bewildered, Ragetti practically stammered, "Brown, what the hell?"

"Don't let your eyes fall out of your head, Ragetti. Good morning Smitty and Patty. I hope you all had a nice vacation. I'm sure I don't have to ask how yours was Ragetti, after all honeymoons are usually the best part of any marriage."

"Yes, sir," they all said in unison. Patty stood up and asked, "Would you like a cup of coffee, sir?"

"Yes, my dear that would be lovely. Now you two come and sit down at this table and I'll tell you what just happened early this morning. Thank God you're both back or I don't know who would have been worthy to take this case. Patty got Brown's coffee and set it discreetly in front of him and returned to her desk. It may be a new procedure for Brown, but at least she would now know what their case would be. It would be fun for Patty if it was always done this way, but she doubted very much the rules would change. Brown had reached his position whereas agents came to him; not the other way around.

As they gathered around the table, Smitty grabbed a pad so he could take notes. It must be a bad one to pull Deputy Director Brown out of his office. And as Smitty took a seat, Brown slapped a photo into the middle of the table. "My God," Ragetti gasped, "isn't that Pope Joseph?"

"I wish I could say no, but you're right, that's exactly who it is. He arrived from Italy two days ago and I believe he was scheduled to leave today. Why, of all the people in this huge city, why did the killer have to choose the Pope? This will have every law agency in the USA getting in on this, it will be chaos, and the public will be in an uproar."

It was all over the news, and it didn't take long before Victoria heard about it. She called Ragetti to see if it would be something that he and Smitty would be working on. Brown had just left their office and of course he had told Ragetti they would be on the case.

Ragetti paused before answering, but knowing how sharp she was he knew there would be no use in lying to his wife. "Yes," he answered in a soft voice. "Of course, as my partner, Smitty will also be involved. I hate cases like this where everyone in the world has an opinion as to what happens, and every department that represents law in this town will be working on this. Not only the people here in Arizona; but Italian officers will want to come and be included in the investigation. Fingers will point, arguments will ensue, and all because of whom the person was that got shot."

"I'm sorry, Sweetheart," Victoria told Ragetti. "I know how you feel about being involved in cases like this."

Ragetti told her "It won't be a good time for anyone in law enforcement, but it's not a surprise that Smitty and I were assigned to look into it. And Brown will have his hands full as it is; with newspapers, TV reporters and probably even the mayor; so someone has to represent the FBI in this shooting, and we are the agents he put in charge. Don't be surprised if I'm late coming home tonight. I can't remember when the last time was that I had to work a case right alongside the Phoenix Police, the CIA and even foreign officers. I can tell you it's not going to be fun. And when it is someone as important as Pope Joseph himself; politics will be involved and everyone will want us to come up with the killer now, not in a week or two, more like two hours from now. And being from Italy won't make it any easier."

There would most likely be several representatives from the FBI present, and it hadn't been decided as yet which office, if any, would take the lead.

It was not clear where the various officers would be meeting, so they just headed to the scene of the crime to see what, if anything; had been discovered thus far. One thing was for sure, with Pope Joseph being killed there would be so many reporters roaming the streets you won't be able to avoid them.

Patty, although feeling very sad about what had just happened, threw herself into gathering facts on the people who were known to be traveling with the Pope. She was Catholic herself, but she couldn't allow herself to drift into wondering how this would affect the church overall. Right now it was her duty to come up with backgrounds. If she ran into anyone with a suspicious background at all she would pass the info on to Ragetti and Smitty.

The headlines were full of information and some papers even had a complete list of all the people included in Pope Joseph's entourage. It seemed strange to her that when a dignitary or anyone who was well-known travelled; it seemed they always took a large group with them. To Patty it seemed the less people you surrounded yourself with the less conspicuous you would be. So it made you wonder, were they looking for the publicity, and it was one way to get it.

As Patty began running the backgrounds of the secondary priests the pattern seemed to pretty much repeat itself. Catholic School was a sure thing, and most had gone into the ministry for training at an early age. They ranged in age from thirty years old to fifty-three for the oldest priest. When she started on the two employees he had brought with him the background wasn't too different. Never any sign of a criminal act and they all seemed to live pure, unexciting lives. All were men and of course it would not have looked at all good to bring a woman along on a very public visit from the pope.

Patty found the backgrounds of the three security guards quite different. But even with them there was no sign of crime or other problems. The only security guard that was married was the oldest one, who had been with Pope Joseph ever since he was voted in as pope. Two of the younger guards had a background of living for several years in the United States. In fact, one of them even had an American father.

Patty turned on the little TV they had in their office. It was seldom used, but in this case she knew every channel would be talking about Pope Joseph, and this would go on until the guilty person was charged and sentenced. Unless, of course, it really was done by a terrorist group. If that was determined, she had no idea how the FBI would fit in.

When the entire group would be allowed to return to the Vatican would depend largely on how willing they were to cooperate with the law. But when you were on your way home there wasn't a person in the world who would be pleased to learn their journey would be delayed for an undetermined amount of time; regardless of what the cause for the delay happened to be. It was just a matter of time before law officials from Italy would begin to arrive. Ragetti looked at the photos that had been taken by the press, by security cameras, and some even by citizens eager to catch a glimpse of Pope Joseph.

This is one place Smitty's uncanny ability to see and remember everything would come in handy.

Back at their own FBI office, Ragetti and Smitty gathered all the photos that had been made. Some were from the press and others were taken from private individuals who had been at the crime scene. The two agents made note of all the men who were in Pope Joseph's group, and painstakingly compared the photos with the names they had access to. It was tedious work, and perhaps useless, but it was the only way anyone could be eliminated of being the shooter. Everyone would have to be questioned, even if the people under suspicion were priests from his own group.

All three security men were easy to spot. They posted one at the rear, one in front and one right beside the Pope, giving the Pope maximum protection. Of course being all three of them were in plain sight at the time of the shooting, they didn't need an alibi.

Whoever did this was a damn good shot, and it had obviously been done at quite a distance. Smitty scanned the buildings nearest the hotel but until he had spoken with the Medical Examiner he had no way of knowing the angle the bullet was coming from.

Smitty told Ragetti, "I think we should talk to the ME's office and see if we can find out the angle the bullet entered the body. Until we know the angle there is too much area to try and interview anyone who may have witnessed the shooting, and there are too many buildings." Ragetti shook his head in agreement and checking with the person in charge of the office they had set up, they found it was only a couple of blocks to the Medical Examiner.

Entering the office of the ME was like entering a conference room milling with people. "Where is the ME?" Ragetti asked a man standing with others in a group. The man pointed to a room adjoining the big entryway. The only thing unusual is that normally the ME and his staff chose to work with as much privacy as possible; but here there was a large picture window where one and all could view the work being done inside the Autopsy Room. It was the first time in all his years of enforcing the law that Ragetti could remember seeing an autopsy being carried out where there was no privacy. Anyone could wander in and look through the large window, even take pictures. It seemed to both him and Smitty that the deceased should be given more respect than to be put on public display. Even people who lived on the streets were given more respect than this.

Smitty turned to Ragetti and asked, "I wonder who authorized this flagrant lack on respect for the deceased?"

"I have no idea," Ragetti answered, "but right now I'm to busy to poke my nose into that hornet's nest."

They knocked and opened the door. As they walked up to the body the ME looked up at them and smiled. "What can I do for you two? Are you FBI or CIA?"

"We're Special Agents Ragetti and Smitty from the FBI" Ragetti announced, "and we were wondering if the angle the bullet travelled had been ascertained as yet?"

"In my opinion it would have come from fairly high up, usually a sniper will position themselves so it's easier to hit the target you want rather than the guy next to him. I would say it came from the fifth floor or higher of a building that would be slightly north of the hotel. I've been to the crime scene and I would guess the most likely building would be the hotel that is adjacent to where the Pope was shot.

Whoever it was had a nice clean shot and hit Pope Joseph right through the heart. The bullet went all the way through the Pope and is probably somewhere in the vicinity of where he was standing. By the way, just for your information, it was a 9-mil judging by the wound."

The ME looked at them and asked if there were any specific questions they had. Ragetti looked at his partner who shook his head, and addressed the Medical Examiner,

"No, I think the information you have supplied will be all that we require for now. How many others have been in to ask you this same question thus far?"

"Actually, no one – kind of surprised me! I thought all the various divisions of the law would be hounding me and maybe even some of the reporters – but no one."

"Thanks, for your information, if you come up with something more, please give us a call," and Agent Ragetti handed him a business card.

The two agents headed back to their office where they could look through all the various photos that had been taken of the crime scene, along with the photos they had taken also. Patty had all the background information of each person in Pope Joseph's organization, with job descriptions, bank account information and a vast amount of information, anything and everything she could dig up.

Ragetti decided to phone the police department and ask if they had completed a thorough sweep of the area surrounding the Pope. According to the ME the bullet had travelled through the Pope's body and was probably lying on the ground somewhere in the area where he had been shot. If a bullet was found Agent Ragetti wanted to know what it was as soon as possible. The Medical Examiner suspected a 9-mil.

As they went through Patty's report on each individual background, they checked them off on the group photo that was taken. Since everyone was dressed almost identical in either a black suit or a priest's robes, it was harder to determine exactly who each one was rather than seeing a crowd with mixed colors of clothing.

Pope Joseph was not hard to identify as he stood out like a sore thumb in all the black garments. He had chosen to wear one of the most colorful vestments that were part of his wardrobe. Patty thought it strange that anyone would dress in garments such as these if they were about to embark on a long plane ride back to the Vatican. At one time in her life Patty had done some volunteer work at her own Catholic Church, and while the vestments were indeed beautiful, she had been shocked when she learned the cost of even some of the plainer robes. And they were also very heavy, not what you would choose to wear on a long plane trip. Perhaps it was all for show and they changed clothes once they had boarded the plane.

Suddenly Smitty pulled out a magnifying glass and looked closely at one of the men standing near Pope Joseph. "This is not the priest we had identified as Father Nicholetti, there are similarities, but I don't believe this is Nicholetti." He magnified each individual person in turn and finally turned to Ragetti and said, "I don't believe Father Nicholetti is present in any of these photos, so where is he?"

Ragetti came over and using the magnifying glass checked out each individual to see for himself if his partner was right. "I'm amazed we missed this the first time around – of course we had no way to zero in on each individual. Father Nicholetti could be our prime suspect."

"Patty let's look at the report on Father Nicholetti and see what his background looks like," Ragetti stated.

All three of them skimmed over the information on this Italian man who had given his life to the church from a very early age. It was not unusual to see he had attended a Catholic School and as soon as he was old enough he went into the seminary. He knew even as a child that he wanted to be a priest when he grew up. And although his record looked good, it seemed that some of the other priests advanced much more rapidly than Nicholetti did.

Patty went back to the computer and in a few minutes she had a list of all the clergy who had been nominated to become Pope back in 2007 when the current Pope was on his deathbed. She was surprised to see Nicholetti's name was on that list. So if he was the guilty party, it could have easily been due to revenge, as he had not been chosen.

Smitty wondered if Father Nicholetti showed up in any of the photos, and checking the ones depicting people pouring out of the hotel, they finally spotted him. He had obviously entered the hotel where they were staying from a side door, and now was hurrying to catch up with his group. Now that they knew who and what they were looking for they could track his progress and saw that indeed,

Father Nicholetti had ended his destination talking to a policeman near Pope Joseph. The ambulance crew was getting the Pope ready to rush to the hospital.

Trying to instill yourself into the crime scene to further prove your alibi was a common act for criminals, it was just quite unexpected in this particular case. Especially if you happen to be Catholic, you like to believe that priests are above such earthly acts of violence. Most people think more about terrorists in situations such as these. They don't expect the murder to have had a personal connection with the Pope and they certainly would never suspect in their wildest dreams that it would be anyone of the Pope's own people.

Terrorists were the first idea that popped into everyone's mind, and considering the alternative, most of the people involved in solving this crime preferred to think that way. Naturally the press picked up on the idea right away, and everyone was feeling very paranoid, thinking there were terrorists running around in the city – it could be the guy next to you, no one knew what to expect. What would be next? Would there be more shootings?

Chapter Two

AGENT RAGETTI STOOD and motioning to his partner, Smitty, he said, "We'd better get as much information as we can from the hotel just to the north of the crime scene. Patty have you determined the name of that hotel yet?"

Patty answered, "The hotel is called The Ridgeway, and I've already put the address on both of your cell phones."

Both agents left the office and Patty continued to use the magnifying glass to further check out photos of the crime scene.

Agent Smitty approached the desk at The Ridgeway and began an idle chat about all the excitement taking place right out in front of them that morning. The clerk had no idea they were FBI and he was eager to tell all he knew. Of course everyone knew Pope Joseph was in the city, and the clerk informed Smitty that he would see them coming and going many times when he was working the front desk.

"Yes, for someone to do this is broad daylight with all kinds of people around it must have been very important to them. To do something so horrible to a foreign dignitary while he was on a good will trip to the United States makes you immediately think it must be a terrorist group. Because if it wasn't a terrorist; that means one of our own people here in the United States may have done it. I understand the entire group was on their way to the airport, so this would have been a last chance type of thing," Smitty commented. "Did you actually see the Pope when he got shot? I wonder exactly where the shooter was located? How did it look to you?"

The clerk paused for a moment and looked at Smitty, "I never really thought about where the shooter was; but it had to be over in this direction somewhere as he was shot from the front, and I have no idea how they did it being he was surrounded by people on all sides."

"Yeah," Smitty agreed – "to get shot in the midst of a crowd like that you'd have to be at a fairly high elevation, so you could be looking down onto the crowd, rather than at ground level where you would only be seeing the tops of people's heads."

Nervously, the clerk looked closely at Smitty again and asked, "Are you the police?"

Agent Ragetti stepped forward and introduced the two of them, announcing "We're FBI Special Agents Ragetti and Smitty. We think the shooter was possibly right in this hotel, so we would like very much to see your list of occupants going back to the time the Pope arrived here, anyone booking in the day before right up until last night, probably from the fifth floor and beyond. How many floors do you have rooms on?

The clerk really looked nervous by now and stammered out his response. "We have, um, twelve floors total and this time of year we are filled practically to capacity. Some guests did leave very early this morning; at least two hours before the Pope was shot, But I will get you the list from three days ago when Pope Joseph first arrived, eliminating anyone who may have checked out before today. In fact, if people checked in a day or two before the Pope arrived and are still here I will include those people also. The register will show you what room they were assigned to and how long they booked the room for. I hope it will help."

"Only guests who had a window looking out on the courtyard are necessary, so if the rooms are not facing the courtyard, please eliminate them. That should narrow it down by a lot," Agent Smitty informed the hotel clerk.

"Does this list show how they paid?" Agent Ragetti asked.

"Yes, normally it is with a credit card, so in case anything is missing or broken we have a way to collect. Maybe one person out of about five thousand will ask to pay in cash."

As the agents waited for the clerk to compile the information, they took a seat in a nearby area, watching the people come and go. They could tell by the décor and amenities within the lobby that this was an upscale hotel. Most people coming here to stay would be well dressed, and if this was planned ahead of time the shooter would know he/she would have to blend in so they did not arouse suspicion.

The hotel had individual coffee flavors to choose from and Agent Smitty helped himself to an exotic sounding blend with a subtle taste of mango. However, he barely had time to take a few sips when he heard the clerk calling their names and approaching them with a large packet.

"This is everything I could find, I even included the people who booked their rooms and are still occupying them, just in case," the clerk told them.

"Thank you, you've been a great help to us. We'll let you know if there is a specific room that we would like to see. And tell the maids to be on the look-out from the fifth floor up and if they see anything that looks suspicious, let us know and cease cleaning that room. We'd hate to have any evidence destroyed by the maid." Smitty smiled at the clerk and they left.

"That worked out much easier than I had anticipated, thank God for your friendly face," Ragetti told Smitty as they made their way to the car.

"Let's get all this information back to the office where we can have Patty sort it by which rooms would be looking out toward the courtyard below. There will be a large number of rooms that can be eliminated just on location alone, although the clerk has eliminated most already."

Patty had not yet gone to lunch when they walked in, so they laid the paperwork down on the round table so they could all observe the layout. Luckily the clerk has been smart enough that he had made a quick sketch showing that rooms 510 through 520, eliminating the odd numbers, would have the best view of the courtyard below. The same held true for the floors above them. They also noticed he indicated sliding doors with a very small patio on about four rooms per floor. That would definitely come in handy.

In the meantime, Patty had already set a block of squares for each floor, with enough room to fill in name, date when booked and planned amount of time staying. As she sat looking at the squares a thought occurred to her,

"Ragetti & Smitty, if I were the shooter and wanted to keep my identity unknown for as long as possible, I would put a "Do Not Disturb" sign on my door and would not show an end of my stay until the next day."

"Patty, you're just too good to be true, sometimes. Thank you, I would not have thought of that, it will help tremendously in narrowing down the rooms we need to investigate. We should call the clerk and tell him we would like to know if any of the rooms put out a "Do Not Disturb" sign this morning, especially on the rooms in question." Smitty made a note of it.

As Agent Smitty had done most of the talking with the clerk he decided he should be the one to call and speak with him, it would speed things up.

When the clerk spoke on the phone, Smitty was surprised to learn he already had more information for them. The clerk had been checking records and found that room 514 had been reserved for two days, but the reservation had been made over two weeks ago. The two days reserved for the room was yesterday, and today, which would give the shooter time to check the layout.

Very excited about all the things they had learned thus far, Agent Ragetti made a quick phone call to the police and also to the CIA to see if they had any new leads. Being those agencies were working on the same case they were agreeable, but both places said that as yet they had nothing that could be considered a 'lead.' So Ragetti decided to make some points and he told them they had been studying the various photos that were taken and discovered the man standing next to Pope Joseph when he was shot was not Father Nicholetti. "They were all dressed so similar we just assumed it was him at first; but using a magnifying glass we could see that we were wrong. We're trying to check where he may have been at the time of the shooting."

The other law enforcement offices were appreciative of this new clue as right now they had no idea at all as to who the shooter was or why the Pope was murdered. Many of the men assigned to the case had no clue where to start looking, and when they heard what the FBI agents had come up with; they felt rather embarrassed to think that none of them had come up with the idea on their own.

Ragetti and Smitty returned to their office and found Patty excitedly looking closely at the crime scene photos.

"I found Father Nicholetti in three different frames that all had the time stamped on them. In the first one he was in the entrance to his hotel, and that was about two minutes from the time of the shot. In the last frame he was talking with the police and standing near Pope Joseph; who was surrounded by ambulance staff. So from the first frame to the last, it took Father Nicholetti exactly three minutes to get within camera range and make his way to the Pope's side. This looks very bad for him."

"Yes, and I think it is time to see if we can set up interviews with the people who were accompanying the Pope; that will include security guards as well as his staff." Ragetti rose and as he was about to head out the door, he looked back at Patty and asked, "Do you know if the entire group is still registered at the Biltmore since the shooting?" Patty gave him an affirmative answer to that and Ragetti and Smitty were on their way.

The lobby of the Biltmore had so many people milling around you would have thought it was a national holiday, but they finally located a clerk who was not otherwise engaged.

Showing him their badges, Ragetti told the clerk "We're investigating the shooting of the Pope and we believe the fatal shot may have come from the hotel to your north, The Ridgeway. We will need to speak with all the individuals who were in Pope Joseph's group. If we could have the room number and name for each one we will ask one at a time to come to the first floor for an interview with us. Do you have a small room we may use for that?"

The clerk immediately agreed to make up the list and handing it to the two agents he said, "Just follow me and I will show you a room that should work perfectly. As the individuals come to the desk I will be able to direct them to this room." At that he stopped and unlocked a room marked "Staff Only" and told them he would have coffee and water brought in and there was a telephone at their disposal to call each individual as they were ready for them.

"This is a perfect setup, thank you so much for your cooperation, Jacques," Smitty smiled at him as he read the name off his uniform.

Jacques smiled back and said, "No problem at all. Let me know when you are through with the room."

Ragetti looked at the list of names the clerk had handed them. "We've got quite a bunch to talk to here. We may as well segregate them and get them done in groups. I have a feeling a lot of them will be a big waste of time. May as well start with security, only three men to talk to there, and Brandon Small is number one. Why don't you call and get him down here, Smitty?"

Smitty picked up the phone and was lucky to have it answered on the first ring. He told Brandon Small who he was and asked him to check with the clerk downstairs to find out the room where they were conducting interviews, and could he please come as soon as possible.

Ragetti glanced at his watch and noting it was two p.m. he decided to call the next man on the list also, so the interviews could be continual. He reached Donald Pinalli and found him agreeable to coming down in fifteen minutes, unless Pinalli received another call from Ragetti and could take him earlier.

There was a knock on the door, Ragetti answered and invited the man in. Brandon Small was a tall, muscular man, with dark hair, who appeared to be in his late twenties or early thirties. The three men introduced themselves and they sat down at the table, each of them had a cup of coffee in front of them.

Ragetti: "Can you just tell us a little bit about yourself Brandon, and let us know how you came to be a security guard for Pope Joseph?"

Small: "I've been in security work ever since I turned twenty-one years old. It seems in Italy there is quite a lot of people who want extra security and can afford to pay for it. I personally applied at the Pope's office for the position even though I didn't know if they were hiring or not. Luck was with me and about six months ago they called and said they had an opening. They wanted to know if I could be ready to start in a week and I told them I could start the next day if they wanted me to. So I'm the newest employee in the Security Department, and the other two guys are great. I trust both of them, and it's a great place to work."

Smitty: "The morning of the shooting did you notice or sense anything being different than all the other times you've left a hotel?"

Small: "Well, I'm the one that brings up the rear and I looked out over the crowd that was gathered. I figured there would be a large group of people gathered trying to get a glimpse of the Pope – this is a Catholic's dream come true, seeing Pope Joseph in person. So, I had been expecting the crowd, but as I glanced over the courtyard and up at the tall buildings surrounding us, I could swear I saw a flash of light from one of the buildings to the north of us. Then I heard the shot and everything turned into chaos."

Ragetti: "Thinking back on it and looking over the surrounding area since then, what area do you think the flash of light came from?"

Small: "I'd say it was from the hotel just to the north of us called The Ridgeway. Everyone was rushing around and I heard the Pope had been shot. I glanced around me to see if the usual people were where they always were, and that's when I spotted Father Nicholetti just exiting the Biltmore and making his way toward Pope Joseph. He is usually stationed right next to him. But I was kept busy controlling the people and I didn't really give it a thought until later."

Ragetti: "Have you been interviewed by the local police, CIA or any other law official before meeting with us today?"

Small: "No, I haven't, which I felt was very strange. I know some of the priests are more comfortable speaking Italian than English, but we were all basically told to go back to our rooms and not to stray far from the hotel. But other than having us all together in the lobby, I believe it was local police doing that; and they asked if anyone had seen or heard anything suspicious and that was it. We were told it was most likely a terrorist and we would be free to fly back to Italy as soon as possible."

Smitty: "And did anyone come and interview you one by one?"

Small: "Not until you guys showed up today. And I know the Italian law representatives are here by now, from Italy, and even they have not been in contact with us."

Ragetti: "We thank you for your cooperation, and I want to compliment you on being sharp on spotting that flash. It was news to us, but we are checking the customers of The Ridgeway right now, and hearing about the flash from that area makes me feel confident we will learn the identity of the shooter fairly soon. You are excused for now." They all shook hands, and even as Brandon Small was heading for the door, there was a quiet knock.

As Brandon opened the door, he recognized Donald Pinalli and told him to come on in. "It looks like you are number two to be interviewed, Donald." And Brandon left.

Security Guard Donald Pinalli looked the role of a guard, muscular, fit, mid-thirties, and he didn't look like someone you would want to mess with. He had a serious look on his face, but when he smiled; his face lit up and changed his looks from serious to friendly.

The two agents asked Donald Pinalli if he would like coffee or water, and he replied cold water would taste good. They settled themselves at the table.

Ragetti: "This is pretty routine questioning, Mr. Pinalli. Just to be completely thorough, would you tell us how long you've been doing security work, and especially how long you have been on the staff for the Pope."

Pinalli: "I have an Italian mother, but my father is American. I was born in Italy but by the age of five we moved back to America. Now I am a citizen of both countries. My father was in the business of security and I joined his company; but my father was killed in a shootout nearly five years ago. When that happened my mother wanted nothing more than to return to Italy to be near her relatives. I was an adult but I chose to return with her.

Smitty: "I guess that explains the blond hair and blue eyes then, you must favor your father in looks; although I must say you certainly have the psyche for a security guard."

Pinalli: "Yes, my mother tells me that often; sometimes I wonder if it is good or bad. It seems to keep him fresh in her memory, and she is still young herself. But I try to look after her and the first thing I did when we settled in Italy was to check on being a security guard for the Pope. Mother and I are both very strong Catholics."

Smitty: "So were you hired on the spot?"

Pinalli: "It was right after Pope Joseph was voted in, and I think he wanted the people who would be closest to him to be of his own choosing. That's why most of us have been there for about six years – at least those of us who are workers, like security, and the Pope's own assistant. He couldn't very well change who the secondary priests were, and there are a few personality clashes, but all in all it's peaceful and friendly."

Ragetti: "What sort of personality clashes are you thinking of? Is there anything of a serious nature?"

Pinalli: "Mostly it was differences of opinion about some of the rules and regulations. For example Father Nicholetti wanted to go exactly by the book and he complained loudly anytime Pope Joseph would make little changes. But he just liked to express his opinion on various things and usually things moved along very smoothly."

Smitty: "Did you notice anything unusual or sense that something was off the morning of the shooting?

Pinalli: "It was a lot more crowded than I had expected, and of course my position is to be on the left-hand side of the Pope anytime we are out in public. I looked around and although everyone was taking photographs, the crowd was fairly calm. I did notice that to the Pope's right there was Father Francis Spinova, he was usually positioned further back."

Ragetti: "Who is assigned to be at the Pope's right side? Are these positions always the same on a trip, and they never vary?"

Pinalli: "In the entire six years of being Pope Joseph's side it has always been the same."

Ragetti: "I think you have been a great help to us, Mr. Pinalli, you are free to go, and I hope you will be on your way back to Italy very soon."

Mr. Pinalli left and the two agents called the third security guard, but allowed themselves a few minutes to straighten out their notes. Both felt very pleased with what had been learned from the two interviews they had conducted thus far, and they both had an eerie feeling of how this was going to play out. Smitty placed the call to Jordan Pinada and he was ready and available, so they asked if he would please come down and check with the clerk for their location and it would be fine if he could arrive in the next ten or fifteen minutes. In the few minutes the agents had to assemble their notes they felt quite sure that the third security guard would prove to give identical information, and he had been in the employment of the Pope ever since Pope Joseph had been in charge. His eyes would have none of the other people in the group blocking his vision, He was right up front.

It did not look good for Nicholetti and it was shocking to both agents to think another priest could be the shooter. It made both Ragetti and Smitty feel slightly sick to their stomach to think of a priest turning against the Pope. How could be go on living knowing what an unforgivable sin he had committed?

Both freshened their coffee and Ragetti turned to Smitty saying, "If this turns out how I think it will I think we should talk to Deputy Director Brown about handing the entire case over to whatever form of law the Italians send over. There will be enough chaos among the people in the United States, especially among the Catholics and we don't really want to drag the name of the FBI into this. Although we may be the ones to find the Pope's killer, I think we should keep a very low profile. I don't care who takes credit for taking the killer down; but I don't want our names splashed across the newspapers taking credit for it."

Smitty knew exactly how he was feeling. People would be looking at them as the two agents who had put a priest behind bars. He agreed with Ragetti to step down if Brown would allow them to do so. But before further discussion could transpire, there was a knock on the door and they knew it would be the last security guard.

"Come in, Mr. Pinada. I'm Agent Ragetti and this is my partner Agent Smitty. You are the last of the security guards for us to talk to and we appreciate very much your cooperation."

"My name is Jordan Pinada, and I suppose I would be considered the senior guard, although Pinalli and I have been employed by the Pope for very close to the same amount of time. If I can think of anything that could be helpful I will be happy to cooperate."

Jordan Pinada appears to be in excellent shape and was probably five to ten years older than the other two guards. And he had a strong Italian accent as he spoke.

Ragetti: "We'll start off the same by you telling us how long you have been in the security business and how long you've been on this particular assignment."

Pinada: "I have spent about eighteen years in this type of business and got into it soon after I was discharged as a Marine. The past six years have been exclusively with Pope Joseph. I am Italian; but was not born in Italy having dual citizenship between Italy and the USA."

Smitty: "Very good, that means you are quite familiar with the rules and regulations of both countries. Although I'm sure it's not an everyday occurrence to have a dignitary shot right next to you. It must seem like a type of nightmare."

Pinada: "I am proud to say that I have never had a person killed while under my guard. I have had close calls, but nothing like this, I always figured it's only politicians who get shot."

Smitty: "What's your take on all this? People who hold down jobs like yours are a great deal more observant than the average person. What did you see, if anything, that would arouse suspicion in you?"

Pinada: "My first thought, and one we were on the look-out for was terrorists. Being away from our own country a terrorist could make an even bigger impact by killing the Pope while we were in the United States. But somehow this doesn't have the right feel to it. First of all a terrorist would have taken credit for the crime by now, they want the fear and apprehension they know they can stir up. I hate to say it but I think it was an inside job, something is off, I just can't put my finger on what it is."

Ragetti: "Did any of the law enforcement gathered at the crime scene show you any of the photographs? They were put in order according to the time stamp on them, and for someone who is familiar with the entire group you may see something that we would miss."

Pinada: "I'm shocked that no one in our entire group has been questioned. I think the law enforcement, although representing many different divisions of the law; all seem to be stuck on the terrorist theory. I've never been on the job when someone as important as the Pope was shot but it seems very strange to me that everyone is concentrating on terrorists."

Smitty: "Would you be willing to come to our office and look over the crime scene photos that were taken? In fact, bring the other two guards with you if you like, the more eyes the better."

Pinada: "We would all like to come look at the photographs, I know Brandon and Donald well enough to know they are as disappointed with the progress and lack of information as I am. May we come over yet this afternoon?"

Ragetti: "This afternoon would be great, call first to make sure we are in our office. Will you require transportation?"

Pinada: "No, the Biltmore has been more than gracious. They take us to any specific place or appointment we may have, and either wait or we call them when ready to come back."

Ragetti: "That's great! We'll see you later then. And thanks so much." The security guard wasted no time in leaving and going to tell the other two guards that they had a chance to examine the crime photos. Being familiar with the entire group perhaps they could spot something out of place.

As for Ragetti and Smitty, they approached the clerk, thanked him and said they were done for the day. "We may be back tomorrow to interview the priests but we are through for today."

At that they left for their office. They had barely gotten back to their office and were still going over the details with Patty when the phone rang. Patty answered and looked questioningly at the agents when the security guards on the phone asked if they could come over in twenty minutes.

Chapter Three

AS THE SECURITY GUARDS filed into the office, Smitty guided the men over to the crime board where all the photos were displayed sequentially.

Patty walked over to the group and Smitty proudly introduced her as Patty, our Researcher. Each guard gave her a big smile and introduced themselves, obviously impressed by her outstanding looks.

Donald Pinalli was the first to point out that in the beginning photos it was Father Spinova standing to the right of Pope Joseph. That's not his usual spot, it should be Nicholetti, Everyone has their regularly assigned spots anytime we're out in public. Over here in the third shot, taken about thirty seconds later, Nicholetti looks like he is just exiting the hotel.

He scanned the remaining photos and said, "Yes, here he is after a minute or so and he's talking with the police. Did any of them talk to either of you about this change of procedure – he certainly did not say anything to me about it."

Both guards Brandon and Jordan said Nicholetti had not spoken to them as they had gathered as a group in the lobby. "In fact," Brandon commented, "thinking back on it I don't remember seeing Nicholetti in the group at all. The Pope likes to give us all a quick blessing before we step out in public, then we turned and exited the front of the hotel."

Ragetti spoke up saying, "I'm sorry I can't discuss any information we have uncovered thus far, as this is an ongoing case, so our lips are sealed. But rest assured with the information we've uncovered from the three of you has taken us a long way toward coming up with the alleged shooter. Have the Italian law enforcement told you anything at all?"

"Not really, they are convinced it is a terrorist act, and they are trying to ascertain exactly the direction the fatal shot came from."

Smitty summed it up by saying "We will tell you this much, we don't believe it was a terrorist attack; we think it was one of your own group. I'm not at liberty to divulge who that individual might be, but it will soon be common knowledge." The security guards left Agent Ragetti and Agent Smitty to ponder what would be the best move to work on next.

Smitty said, "It seems the next step would be to check out the room in The Ridgeway that seems most likely. If we could find some trace that Nicholetti is the one who rented the room we'd have proof that couldn't be ignored. And who knows what we may actually find in the room."

Ragetti moved for the door and talking over his shoulder said, "You've got me thinking just like you, I'm sure a thorough investigation of the room, namely 514, will end up turning up some evidence that will narrow down who is responsible. Let's get on it."

Smitty approached the clerk with a friendly smile on his face. "I'm Agent Smitty with my partner Agent Ragetti, we're from the FBI. We would like access to room 514 which we have already been speaking with a different clerk regarding this; and he gave us the reservation schedule and layout of the rooms. It's in connection with the Pope being shot." The clerk looked at them with suspicion.

"What if our customer is in his room right now? I could get in serious trouble if I let you in a room that's under someone's name, and he could even be in the room as we speak."

"Call the room and see if anyone answers. Then give us the passkey so we can check it out. If there is any problem that comes of this, we will take full responsibility."

The clerk dialed room 514, and of course there was no answer. He still looked very nervous; but he handed over the passkey. Ragetti grabbed it and they took off for the elevator.

Sure enough, room 514 had a "Do Not Disturb" sign on the door. Ragetti knocked loudly on the door as he yelled: "FBI – OPEN THE DOOR!" No answer, so they used the passkey and entered. The bed was neatly made and a chair had been pulled over to the patio door. A gun lay on the floor and the patio door was still slightly ajar.

Smitty bagged the gun and looking at Ragetti said, "Want to bet there are no fingerprints on this?"

Ragetti laughed and answered, "I don't make bets if I'm not sure of winning. Let's get this over to the lab. I think the CIA could get Father Nicholetti's fingerprints from Italy quicker than we could, so it's time to do some more sharing."

They took the passkey back to the clerk and told him NOT to have the room cleaned. It would be better if the maid did not go in as there was bound to be some fingerprints somewhere in the room.

Off to the headquarters they had set up as a temporary measure, and this time Ragetti asked to see the Head CIA Agent. A tall man with a muscular build looked over at them and had overheard what they said.

He approached Ragetti and Smitty and held out his hand saying, "I'm Daniel Black, I guess I'm the one you want to talk to."

Ragetti and Smitty both shook his hand and introduced themselves. "Is there somewhere private where we can talk?" Ragetti asked.

"Sure, just follow me." He led the way to a small room with no windows, but there was a large mirror on the wall and in it they could see all the agents and individuals gathered in the big room they had entered from. "Sometimes it's nice to be able to observe the people who are working on the case" the CIA agent announced as he sat down.

Ragetti explained their background, mainly how The Ridgeway had been targeted as the most likely place the shooter had been located. "To make a long story short, we just came from there and talked the clerk out of the passkey for room 514. There was a "Do Not Disturb" sign on the door and no visible signs of occupancy. The patio door was ajar and this gun was lying on the carpet near the door." At that he laid down the evidence bag and said the CIA should get a team up there to look for fingerprints or some clue of the shooter that could have been left behind.

The agent looked at them with admiration, and told them "We heard the two guys from the FBI were hot-shots; but I never expected this. Who is your prime suspect, I'm sure at this point you probably have one."

"Yes, we think the man you're looking for is Father Nicholetti. We noticed the time stamp on the photos and saw the priest next to Pope Joseph at the time of the shooting was not Father Nicholetti, as we had first assumed. Checking further we found it would take him approximately three minutes to get from The Ridgeway to the Biltmore, entering from the side and making his way to be near the Pope and start talking to the police. He thought it would give him an airtight alibi; but all it did was incriminate him. It's just our opinion, of course."

Ragetti took a deep breath and glanced over at Smitty. "It was actually in our office when we first noticed the mistaken identity of the man next to the Pope as he was shot. Nicholetti was like second in command, and it was assumed by all of us that he would be at the Pope's side. But as we started examining the faces of each person it was obvious that the priest next to Pope Joseph was not Father Nicholetti."

Smitty folded his hands and sat back.

Agent Black looked at them in amazement. "I can't believe that the two of you have done all of this research and what you've come up with. Most of the other divisions of the law are still talking about how it had to be terrorists to plan something like this. What made you even suspect one of the Pope's own people?"

"Well, like I said," Ragetti answered, "when we looking at the photographs with a microscope it became obvious that the Pope's people were not in their assigned positions. To me they all looked too much alike, I don't know any of them, and they were all dressed in black – so it's easy to be confused."

"I'll be damned!" Black just stared at them. "Do you have any opinion about how this whole thing should be handled?"

Ragetti looked Agent Black right in the eye and told him"I say we should turn all the evidence we've uncovered over to the Italian law division, let them take it back to Italy to deal with it. If we arrest Nicholetti and throw his ass in prison here; all of Italy and many other countries will be up in arms about it, especially people who are Catholic. We won't look like heroes -- we'll be treated like villians!"

Black agreed with Ragetti and said as slow as the wheels of justice turn it would most likely be tomorrow before they got a call back on fingerprints; but he said he would send a crew over to sweep the room at The Ridgeway immediately. And he promised to keep in touch.

As Ragetti and Smitty headed back to their own office they both breathed in a big sigh of relief "Tomorrow is Friday and I think it will be the end of the case," both said simultaneously. Glancing at his watch and noting it was nearly quitting time he said he thought it would be a good idea to stop by and go over the details with Brown.

Before we can try turning this over to anyone we need to know what his thoughts are. Some of the agents had already left for home, but Ragetti approached the desk, giving his name and saying he needed a quick word with Deputy Director Brown. The officer kind of raised his eyebrows, but he picked up the phone and dialed Brown's extension. The message was brief and the answer even briefer – Brown came to the door and beckoned them in.

"For God's Sake, does everybody sit and watch the clock all day so they don't miss a single minute of their off time, or is it just these goons who work for me who do that?" Brown slammed a book down on his desk and told the boys to have a seat. "At least you aren't clock watchers or you would have waited until morning to do this. Thank God there are still a few of us left who go home when the job is done. Let's have some good news to end up the day."

Ragetti filled his boss in on all that had taken place in the past couple of days and ended by telling him how the gun was in the room that would have been ideal for the shooters location. They said the general consensus among the various divisions of the law was that it had to be a terrorist to blame for this. So strong were their feelings not even one of the various divisions had taken the time to speak with the people in Pope Joseph's group. As of right now I'm ninety-nine percent sure the guilty one is Father Nicholetti. I don't like it, but those are the facts and it's my opinion the way it should be handled is to let the Italian Law Dept. have all the evidence we've turned up and let them take Nicholetti to Italy and settle it there. Lots of people in the world will be up in arms over this so it's a good time to keep a low profile. Let Italy handle it. This isn't the time to be the hero, let's just hand it over and let it go. Of course we will do whatever you want as you're the boss."

"Dammit, you hand me good news then snatch it right away! I could just see us gloating over our victory while the rest of the idiots set talking about a terrorist. I should have known there would be a down side to this. I hate to admit it but I think you're right, nobody will love us and admire our intelligence in solving this case; we would just be remembered as the law group that accused a priest of murdering Pope Joseph, and that would take a long time to go away.

As soon as you get your evidence together ask the head of the Italian law group and Agent Black from the CIA to come and see me and I will inform him how it will be handled. Just bring me the evidence and reports to back this up."

Chapter Four

THE CIA WAS TELLING the truth when they said they didn't move too fast, but Ragetti was expecting that on a case of this caliber, everyone involved would be working through the weekend, just like any other day. But just to make sure Ragetti had phoned the office that was set up just for the case dealing with Pope Joseph; all he reached was a recording that said briefly that the investigation was underway and if anyone had further information please call 800-555-5555.

So if it wasn't that big of a hurry to the police, the CIA or even the Italians, then the FBI may as well take the week-end off also. There was nothing to move forward with until the report from the room sweep came back. Finding some trace of Father Nicholetti was the missing piece of the jigsaw puzzle.

Ragetti turned to his bride and said it looked like they had a free weekend; no one was working on the case, and of course Victoria was off for the weekend as usual. "So how would you like to spend the day, Sweetheart?"

Victoria stretched and yawned, "I'd like to spend the morning going through the house and checking to see if there is anything left that I need to buy and also check to make sure we didn't gather a bunch of dust while on vacation.

But for the afternoon I'd love to invite Susan, Smitty and the boys over to hang around the pool and Susan and I can fix up some snacks. We might even want to barbeque later in the afternoon. If we need anything from the store we can always see if Patty will go."

"That sounds like a plan to me. In fact while you're checking out the house I think I will mow the lawn front and back. May as well let the neighbors know right from the start that we're not trying to keep up with the Jones, I can do yardwork also."

"Let me get breakfast fixed, then I'll see what Patty is up to. After we've eaten you can enjoy your outdoor time. Just be happy that it still hasn't reached triple digits outside; I have a feeling you might change your mind about doing your own yardwork once that hits."

Patty came down to help her sister with breakfast and said she would help check the rooms and see if there was any cleaning to be done. Victoria told her they probably should check their grocery supply as she wanted to invite the Smitty family over for swimming in the afternoon – which could entail a grocery run for supplies. Patty said she would be happy to do the grocery run as she had a couple of errands to do anyway. Breakfast was delicious and they all gobbled down the golden waffles Victoria had come up with; complete with bacon and milk to drink. Of course she made fresh coffee also as she knew she'd want her morning coffee as she was looking through the house.

When Victoria called Susan, Susan said, "Of course we'd love to come over and swim. It seems like months since we've seen one another instead of three weeks. Shall I put together a couple of snacks to bring over?"

Victoria said that would be greatly appreciated and outlined her plans for the morning. "Just think how lucky we are to have Ragetti and Smitty home with us this week-end when they're right in the middle of such a big case. Rigatti has hardly said a word about the case, did Smitty tell you anything?"

"Not a word. I've gotten to where I don't even ask anymore. You'll soon find out it does no good to ask an FBI agent any questions until they're ready to talk; and by that time you may as well just read about it in the newspaper or watch it on TV." Susan laughed.

By one thirty everything was set, Lots of towels out by the pool, two ice chests filled with wine coolers, beer and soda and there were two appetizers ready to come out of the oven. Thank God she had seen that sale on chaise lounges at The Patio Shop shortly before their vacation was to start, she had ordered several, a few chairs, and a couple of tables. Looking around she was very happy that the previous owners had moved out of state and had left behind all the lush pots of plants, flowers and bushes. It looked like an oasis out here; and a very private on at that. As she surveyed the back yard she decided that a nice water feature would look good. With the day temps in Arizona she was glad the patio was nearly completely covered and as a bonus there were even mesh type of shades that could be lowered in strategic areas.

The doorbell chimed and she ran for the door. Susan entered first and they threw their arms around each other. Smitty stepped in and noticed Ragetti coming down the stairs wearing a pair of shorts and still rubbing his hair with a towel. The boys barely bothered to say 'hello' to anyone before they were out the door and heading for the water.

After everyone was exhausted from swimming and playing a version of volleyball, they relaxed in the lounge chairs and Smitty, who was always hungry, wanted to know if they were planning on having a barbeque.

Ragetti said, "I'm sorry, I forget you're a bottomless pit. It just happens that Patty, smart little gal that she is, picked up a 6-foot long Subway and we've got hot dogs and buns to throw on the grill. So it's your choice."

Patty piped up to say, "Don't forget there is potato salad and baked beans too."

Victoria looked lazily over at Susan and said, "Let's let the men handle this for a change and we'll just relax and have another wine cooler. Patty can help them if they really get stuck." Susan agreed, and turning to her husband she told him, "It's your turn, honey, so you and your partner just get busy setting everything up. Go ahead, you'll do fine. Right now I think I'm in heaven and I couldn't move even if I wanted to."

Ragetti got up and pulling Smitty to his feet by his hand he grumbled, "We wouldn't be in this situation if you didn't have food on your brain all the time."

Once Ragetti and Smitty got into the spirit of setting everything up, they found it wasn't all that hard after all. Paper plates for easy clean-up; but real silverware because they knew the wives would balk if they went too far, and of course real glasses.

It wasn't long before Patty came out to see how things were going. She added napkins, condiments and a big bouquet of sunflowers. The hot dogs were on the grill, Subways were piled high on a giant platter, and she let them get away with leaving the potato salad and baked beans in the containers. "I think you guys did a great job for beginners," Patty grinned at them. "I will go in and tell the Queens that the food is ready."

Everyone enjoyed the impromptu food that had been put together, and Victoria said, "You know, I could spend every week-end like this."

The boys cheered and said they wanted to come over every day, but seeing their mom, Susan frowning at them they added, "But even the week-ends would be a treat."

Susan turned to Victoria and with a smile said, "It was good of you to invite us all over when you've barely gotten back from your honeymoon. I know having six people come barging into your home can't be the best way to relax and enjoy the day – but I want you to know we all enjoyed it so much, it's like being in a fancy resort to come over here."

Victoria laughed, "I wouldn't say it's that special, but the good thing is, you won't get a bill when you're ready to leave."

Susan burst out laughing over that one and said she promised to make it up to them by cooking some delicious meals. "Let me get my boys rounded up and we'll talk again later. By the way, I love the way you've decorated the house so far. When in the world did you have the time to do furniture shopping?"

"I can make up my mind pretty quickly, so I just went into a store that I like, made notes and after about an hour I had almost everything you see here picked out. And of course there is always online shopping, I love it," Victoria told her.

As they all said their goodbyes and gave hugs, it suddenly seemed very quiet in the house and Patty spoke up, "I know what we need – a dog!"

"Hold that thought for a while, sis, I'm not sure I'm ready for a pet yet," Victoria sighed. "I don't know about you two; but I'm worn out. Swimming, doing the lawn, it has me zapped right down to zero energy. It is nap time for me,"

Ragetti said. "And I'm going to join you!"

Victoria laughed as she ran up the stairs. Just as she reached the top of the stairs she heard Ragetti's cellphone ring. "And I hope this has nothing to do with the case you're working, let's not spoil the weekend.

Ragetti picked up his phone "Ragetti speaking."

"This is Agent Black from the CIA. Sorry to disturb your evening, but the news just came in that Father Nicholetti's fingerprints were found in two separate places in room 514. One of the places was the toilet flush handle, and the other place was on the cord to adjust the blinds. Not actually on the cord itself, but on the knob at the end of the cord. It looks like there is no other conclusion but to see Father Nicholetti as the prime suspect. What do you want me to do next? I mean the FBI, you and your partner in particular, are the ones who solved this."

Ragetti sighed and said, "I'm sorry it turned out this way. Somehow it would have been better if it had been a terrorist, you know? But what you need to do now is get in touch with my boss; that would be Deputy Director Brown. We've already discussed this and the situation can better be handled between the two of you. Have a nice weekend, goodbye for now."

"Goodbye, enjoy your weekend, Ragetti. It was a pleasure working with you."

Ragetti hung up the phone and flopped down on the bed. "It looks like our big hot case has been solved. Sorry to say all the evidence points to Pope Joseph being shot by one of his own priests."

Victoria looked at Ragetti and had lots of questions to ask; but seeing the look on his face and the sadness in his eyes, decided the questions were not important after all.

Ragetti did not even tell Smitty until the next morning. Even then he still felt sick to his stomach; and he knew that Smitty would not take the news lightly. He told Victoria he didn't feel like eating and would just have coffee. "Do you want to take a ride over to Smitty's so I can tell him this in person?

"Sure Sweetheart, I think that's a great idea!" And off they went. As they pulled up to Smitty's house Victoria said she hoped they were both up.

Ragetti looked at her and laughed, "With four boys I think it's pretty likely they have both been up for hours."

Susan opened the door and looked surprised at seeing Ragetti and Victoria. "What's the matter, Victoria tired of cooking for you already? But she noticed the serious look on both of their faces, and she said "Smitty is in the living room," as Victoria walked her into the kitchen.

"Hey Fella! What's up? It's been a long time since I've seen you over here on a Sunday morning." Smitty looked up laughing, but seeing the look on his partner's face his smile was wiped off his face.

"I wish I didn't have to tell you this bad news, Smitty. God! It was bad when we had to solve the Medicare Scam and find out some of our friends were involved. And last night the CIA agent called to tell me the sweep had turned up two sets of Father Nicholetti's fingerprints—he is obviously our killer. I referred him to Brown; but I couldn't call and tell you news like that on the phone." They both put their head into their hands, and when they finally sat up and looked at each other, their eyes were wet.

Smitty hugged Ragetti. "Thanks partner, another case I wish we had never been assigned to. Is this job really worth it?" Without waiting for an answer he walked into the kitchen and poured himself a cup of coffee. "Have you guys eaten yet, Susan has a delicious casserole in the oven, and we'd love to have you join us?"

Ragetti looked over at Victoria and saw she gave him a slight nod, so he said, "Sure, it sounds great – it's been a while since we've seen you guys!"

"That's my partner alright, always has a smart answer," but Smitty was grinning. When they were finally ready to go back home, both Ragetti and Smitty felt calm and collected again. They were still sad, but they were glad this case was over and also that they would not be the ones having to interview and question Father Nicholetti. How could they even feel comfortable addressing him as "Father" after the sin he had committed? The phone rang and Smitty picked it up.

"FBI Agent Smitty, how may I help you?" A giggle came over the phone and Smitty immediately felt his day brighten. "Mai, is it really you? How are you doing?"

"It's a little early to be telling you about it, but I'm so excited I had to tell somebody or go crazy – I'm having my own art show in a month. I can hardly believe it. I did phone Mr. Chan already and his entire family is coming, even Michelle. What started out as such a sad and terrifying situation has ended up turning my life around! I couldn't be happier. I hope all of you can come, bring your family and of course Agent Ragetti and don't forget to tell Patty, she is the first one to show me such kindness."

Smitty hung up the phone with a big smile on his face. This was wonderful news, and the fact that Mai was having her own art show just proved she was on her way to success. He could not wait to let the whole team learn of this good news. He immediately turned to Ragetti to let him know, he knew the whole team would want to go. "Victoria, when you get home tell Patty that she received a special invitation from Mai, as she remembers her as one person that was especially kind to her while she was here."

When Victoria and Ragetti arrived back at their own home, Victoria called to Patty, "Come on down, Patty, I have some great news for you."

"It's good there is some good news, it seems this week has had enough bad events so I don't want to hear anything bad," Patty said.

Victoria told her the news about Mai and Patty did her little happy dance. "I can't believe what I'm hearing. This is kind of like a fairy tale. Mai was poor and had terrible things happen to her when she was still a young teen. I just can't imagine knowing your parents had been killed, and raped the very same day. To top it off she came to America by trusting the wrong person and her life in hell really hit her. I don't even want to think of the things she had to endure. And now she has a benefactor and a mentor – along with her own art show. It's just like becoming a fairy princess. And now I'll get to actually see and talk with Mai."

Monday morning came and although all three of them were right on time; none of them looked too happy. And no one really wanted to talk about it either. Patty said she'd like to go over to the Office Supply Department and pick up a few things they needed. She knew the guys would just as soon be alone so she would take her time.

Chapter Five

SMITTY DECIDED TO WAIT until Tuesday's staff meeting to fill in the other people. There had been a lot of surprises last weekend, and all of them were good. What a great way to end the week. That would be a week that he would always remember, and most likely a lot of other people too, due to Pope Joseph being killed.

Ragetti simply said, "I love the ones that have a happy ending; but we're in the wrong business for it be the normal, Thank God we have one of those rare endings once in awhile, it helps keep us all on track."

Patty, always the practical one said, "I'm going to make sure our records of the Pope Joseph's case are in good shape; I don't want a single fact to be out of order. And I'll bet anything the next time you hear from Brown he will want you both to write up a full report. I have a feeling today is going to be our paperwork day – at least I hope it is, I'm not sure I'm ready for another traumatic case so soon.

Ragetti told them he had picked up a newspaper this morning to see if the press had any news given to them about how things would be handled. And lo and behold there it was on the front page. "Killer of Pope Joseph was one of his own priests." This would probably continue on for a week or so, and even then there were some people who would grumble about it. Nothing could ever suit the entire public, no matter how it was handled. Ragetti and Smitty both began the lengthy process of writing their reports so they could have that out of the way.

"We should have them finished by lunch time, so what do you say we all go out to lunch together?" Smitty asked. Both Ragetti and Patty answered with a loud YES! It was good to have a somewhat normal day to look forward to. Not one of them grumbled about the paperwork as they were all so happy not to be in the middle of a high-stress case.

Brown had also looked at the morning newspaper and was glad to see that Ragetti and Smitty were not mentioned specifically as being the ones to solve the case. All the people who had been in the Pope's staff were on their way back to Italy. All were glad to get back to their normal lives, and hoped the scandal would not go on forever. Then there would be all the news of the Vatican choosing a new Pope, so it would be months before things settled down.

Brown received a call that would require him to send out two special agents; but knowing what Ragetti and Smitty had just been through, he assigned it to two other agents. He could only imagine the turmoil Ragetti and Smitty were still going through. His phone rang and it was Patty on the other line. "Hi Patty, are you looking for a new job to do?" and he laughed.

Patty assured him she was happily catching up on paperwork, and both of the agents were busy working on their reports; which would be turned in right after lunch. "I actually have some good news to share with you. Smitty received a call from Mai on Sunday night and she was so excited to tell him she is going to have her own Art Show, she will be the featured artist; and of course she is hoping that all of us from here will come to Los Angeles to help her celebrate."

"I love getting good news, Patty, so thank you for calling me. I'm sure there are several people from here who will plan on attending. Goodbye for now and have a nice day."

It was now Wednesday and although it was nice to have some time to relax and feel normal again, both Agent Ragetti and Smitty were getting a little antsy about getting on with business. Theirs was not the type of job where they had the luxury of sitting around drinking coffee.

Ragetti finally picked up the phone and called his boss, Deputy Director Brown. "It's been great having a couple of days to relax and catch up; but now I'm starting to get cabin fever. I've been sitting around in this office too long; don't you have something exciting to get us out of here?" Ragetti asked Brown point blank.

Brown laughed, "You know, I wondered how long it would take you to call. In fact, I had a call from our buddies up North, Sedona to be exact. I've just been trying to decide if I should forget about it, or follow through on it."

"What? I can't believe you would say that! You've never looked the other way on a case in your entire life. What's so special about this one?" Ragetti was curious.

"Come on over and bring Smitty with you, let's see what you think." And Brown hung up the phone.

"What's he got?"Smitty chimed in.

"Damned if I know, he loves being able to drive a person crazy by just hinting at things, but he wants us both over at his office pronto." Ragetti headed for the door.

Everything was quiet around Brown's office and it seemed a little eerie not to see everyone hard at work. Brown opened his door and he waved them on in. "Sit down, gentlemen, and make yourself a cup of coffee if you like. It might take a bit to explain what I know so far; which isn't a hell of a lot." Brown slumped in his chair.

The agents had their coffee and settled down, what could possibly be so mysterious?

Brown sipped on his coffee and turned to stare out of the window. "Have either of you ever been to Sedona?"

"Of course" the agents answered in unison.

"Well, the story I get from Sheriff Bauer is that things could have been going on for about a week or even two. Some people run right to the police, but as you know in Sedona, Policemen and even the Sheriff are not very noticeable in the throngs of thousands of tourists."

Brown went on to tell the story, "About ten days ago a tourist called 911 and said that his partner had gone for a early morning walk and had never returned. They had things planned for the day so it was not like him to just disappear with no word. The police found the man's car at a parking lot below one of the trails, locked and the keys were missing. Naturally they put out an alert and even had dogs out looking around the trail he had taken, but nothing was found. The dogs got a little excited at one point, so they must have picked up a scent, but from there on it went cold. To this day he has not been found, and no one has seen or heard from him."

"It would sound strange for a guy to do it in that manner if he wanted to go away and get lost for awhile." Smitty observed "and especially since he wasn't in Sedona alone. What did the person or people he left behind have to say about it?"

"He said his partner would never just take off like that. He was a happy man and was even planning on getting married in a couple of months. His girlfriend has heard nothing from him either."

"The sheriff and the police searched for two or three days and had about given up at this point when another call comes in about a small group that had climbed up Cathedral Mountain. The hike went well, but on the way down, one member said he was going to hang back a bit so he could catch some of the sunset views. He would see them at the hotel. Again, the group waited until it was time to go out to dinner and he still had not returned. They tried his cell but with no response. Finally they went to eat and decided they would call the police if he still was not back after dinner. He wasn't back, and that's when they called."

"So far that's two people missing in less than a week." Ragetti observed. "What do the locals say, or do they even know?"

"According to the sheriff there isn't much talk about it so far, but that will change soon, our kidnapper or killer as it may be is stepping up his action. In the time since it first started there have been three more missing people, and worse yet, a leg was found on one of the popular trails. Upon examination by the ME at a local hospital they think it was a woman, white, and not too old judging by the skin, probably in her twenties or early thirties I don't believe upon reading the description of the other three missing persons that the woman was one of them. There is still no word on her, and worse yet, no way to identify her."

Smitty interrupted to say "In what manner was the leg cut off? There should have been a lot of blood, and there is no easy way to cut through the bone that close up to the hip."

Brown looked distressed as he told them there was no blood splatter, nothing that looked like there could have been a battle, nothing at all – just the leg. As inexperienced as the M.E. was he did say there were some unsure cuts on the leg, and then the killer must have switched to a saw. I know I can't just ignore this and think it will stop. But Sedona has a wacky reputation as it is, yes it's beautiful, but there are some very weird people living in the area.

Brown went on to tell them that policemen had questioned a few people who lived around the area where they disappeared; and they came back with stories that are beyond belief. He sat there looking at the two agents who were looking at each other.

To tell the truth it made Smitty's skin crawl, and it made him half believe it was all an elaborate hoax. But unless you were some kind of crazy person or a monster, who would find something like this funny?

"Have any locals been attacked or reported in any of these incidents? That would be other than the lady whose identity was not known, of course. And if she was local you would think for sure someone would be calling in." Ragetti speculated.

Brown looked very serious as he spoke, "I want you Agent Ragetti and Agent Smitty to drive up to Sedona, we have a motel room all booked for you. You will be more or less undercover so people will be more apt to talk to you, you are both journalists and your job is to write about the mystic of Sedona. There is a lot of talk about magic, voodoo, aliens, and the popular notion of vortexes. The fortune tellers gather around on the week-end to lure you in. It may sound like a paid vacation to some, but I wouldn't want the job if you paid me double. This could be very dangerous, so I would prefer you go up without your families, and don't tell them much about what's going on. You never know what or who you might be dealing with when the person is crazy or alien. You can tell Patty of course, and she will be here available to look things up on the computer for you."

"I know Patty is very good at piecing things together, so she will keep meticulous notes and looking with her gut instinct and knack of spotting something out of the ordinary she will still be more of an asset here than there. Besides I have a rule about putting civilians in danger."

"When do you want us to leave?" Ragetti asked.

"NOW," Brown answered curtly. "Pack a few tourist type clothing, maybe a pair of slacks and a couple of open at the collar shirts and don't forget to carry a small pad or a tape recorder with you everywhere you go. You'll be from a little magazine called "Learn the Truth Here" and each of you will have business cards, but with your regular cellphone numbers on them. Better take your vest and a uniform too, just in case you arrest the maniac."

"Ragetti, your name in the undercover job will be Paul Dodson, and you Smitty will be David Erickson. You'd better get used to hearing the name Paul and David because that's who you are now, unless you are speaking with the law, with them you can use your real names."

At that they both left, went to their office to fill in Patty, then on home to pack. They agreed to take Ragetti's car and Smitty's car would be left at his house.

Chapter Six

ON THE DRIVE UP BOTH were browsing through their own thoughts. What would they discover in the hill, valleys and mountains of the 'red rock country' Ragetti didn't believe in aliens, but some of the things that science was starting to investigate and come up with did leave him a little on the shaky side. Smitty on the other hand followed all the science fiction shows on TV and was a big fan of "X-Files." He didn't want to meet one of them in person though. In all seriousness, this was a far cry from a vacation in woo-woo land.

On the way through the Village of Oak Creek they stopped and ate lunch. The restaurant was quite crowded as it was nearing noon. Just what they needed. The more people the better. More people meant more stories. They made sure everyone could hear them say they were journalists and wanted to write about the real Sedona. What about the vortex spots? Were they for real or just a spooky story?

By the time they had finished their lunch they had quite a crowd around their table, some tourists, and a few locals. People were eager to talk about anything they had heard, seen or even speculated about. One woman approached them and said something a little strange had happened to her about two weeks ago. She wanted to know if they wanted to hear the story.

Smitty told her "Yes, we are interested in all the various stories people care to share with us. So please tell us what happened to you."

"My name is Mildred, just so you know, and a couple of weeks ago I decided I would try a fairly easy trail, it's to the West of Uptown. I probably shouldn't have gone alone, but my friends say I'm so slow they don't like to walk with me. Anyway I was about halfway up the path when I lost my footing and started to slide down the hill, heading back in the direction I had just come from. There was a drop off to my left and I was sure I would plunge to my death at any moment. I was sliding on the seat of my pants."

Smitty urged her to continue.

"Well, there was a slight curve ahead and I figured that's where I would slide off the trail and plunge to my death. Suddenly there was a man that came around the corner and sat down in the middle of the path with his back facing me. There was no way I could stop, my hands, legs, and arms were already all cut and scratched, there was blood everywhere. So of course the inevitable happened and I crashed into the man, my legs actually straddled him and it gave us both quite a jolt."

"He stood up, brushed himself off and helped me to my feet. He had a cloth with him and proceeded to wipe my arms and legs with it, getting most of the blood off me. Then he turned and looked at me."

"What are you doing out here alone? You have no water with you, and the shoes you have on are not fit for hiking. Had I not been close at hand, you'd probably slid off the trail and be dead by now. This is not a safe place to be out walking alone. Go home now and don't try to hike again unless you are properly equipped and always bring water plus at least one other person."

Mildred hugged herself and continued talking, rather shakily "It's like he was giving me a direct order, but I was sore and half scared to death. I didn't argue with him; I just said thank you for helping me and started back down the trail. After a few feet I stopped and looked behind me but there was no sight of him."

Ragetti asked her if she could describe the man and she said his face was imprinted on her brain.

"He was quite tall and professional looking. He had dark hair with a few silver hairs starting to show through. He looked to be in excellent shape and probably hiked a lot. But although he had helped me, probably even saved my life, he was kind of scary. Like he had no emotions and it was a nuisance to come across me on the trail."

"That was an interesting experience, Margaret, and we both thank you for sharing it with us. Now if you will excuse us, we need to get checked into our motel. Goodbye everyone."

Pulling into their motel, they were pleased with the location. It was the fork between Hwy 179 and Hwy 89, with a huge shopping center directly across from them and every other building seemed to house a restaurant. They had a room toward the back with a small patio so they could watch the people come and go from the uptown area. Thinking ahead they had stopped at a small grocery store in the Village of Oak Creek and stocked up on crackers, cheese and lunch meats, beer naturally, and Smitty, the practical one, grabbed a couple tomatoes, bread and some mayo. On second thought he added cereal and milk. Most places offered breakfast, but cereal was always a good late night snack too. He wasn't used to traveling and having to think what to buy because Susan was always with him and she handled that stuff.

Neither was really hungry, so they put away their stash of groceries and sat down to have a beer and hash things over between them.

Ragetti started, "OK let's really think out of the box and say there's an alien here in town; maybe more than one. What benefit would it do them to get the town riled up by kidnapping people? Do you think they want to study a few people to see how far we've advanced?" He chuckled as he added the last part.

Smitty of course responded in defense of the alien theory, "You can laugh about it if you want, but there are many things in our past that cannot be explained with anything or anybody who would be more likely than aliens. They are far advanced from people on Earth, but I do not think this has to do directly with the aliens; but perhaps will someone who believes in them with all his heart and soul. He will come across a little crazy to most people because most of his ideas and conceptions are completely out of the box. Whatever his reasoning, he certainly picked the right town to do it in. When people hear about this they will gobble it up."

"It could be someone who thinks it's a lot of fun to scare people, and what better than a spooky little town with lots of out-of-state visitors milling around at all times? All he would have to do is kidnap three or four people and the town would be scared to death. I think most of the people who actually live in Sedona are attracted by two things; first the beauty of the area, and secondly for the mystic that surrounds the area," Ragetti added. "Let's see if we can get out talking to some of the locals.

The restaurants should be slow by now and lots of waiters and waitresses are eager to share their knowledge. Let's hear some of the exciting stories they will love to share with us. Be sure we bring our journals.

And off they went in search of a cozy place with lots of people to talk to. As they sat enjoying a delicious enchilada, Smitty signaled to the waitress. Naturally she hurried right over. "I don't mean to take up all of your time, but we're a couple of journalists and are here to gather folk lore, debunk myths, learn about vortexes and all the other stuff that Sedona is famous for. Do you have any personal story of something that has happened to you that you could tell us about? If you get called away, we'll wait for you to come back. And by the way, what's your name? We're journalists from a little paper called "Learn the Truth Here." My name is Paul Dodson and this is my associate David Erickson."

The waitress told them her name was Suzanne and she had a very strange experience with her neighbors right after moving to Sedona. My husband, Steve and I, found a house right here in what's called 'uptown' and it didn't take us long to put in an offer. We had never heard of javalina or coyotes as we were used to living in a dense city population and one night we went sightseeing, leaving our dogs tied up in the yard.

When we got home it had just gotten dark and we found our two neighbor ladies had our dogs and scolded us for leaving them at this time of day. They said "Don't you know this is the time of night the coyotes and javalina come right down this road and on through your yard?"

Of course we had a stupid look on our face and asked "What are javalina?"

The two ladies looked at us with scorn. "They are like wild pigs and although they can't see very well, they have a keen sense of smell. And speaking of smell, they are foul smelling animals and they could tear your dogs into pieces with their long tusk-like teeth. You need to try and keep your dogs indoors once it is dusk."

We thanked them and lost no time in getting our dogs inside the house. These two ladies were a little strange, but we knew nothing about Sedona, and we had already been forewarned that there were some really weird people hanging around town. The ladies seemed to be friendly; both were slim, had platinum blonde hair and must have been six feet tall or more. They told us their names were Lane and Sue Thornton. Day by day they would say a few words to us and one day the one asked me if I'd like to know what they did for a living.

I was very curious as I knew the rent on a house as nice as theirs would not come cheap, and neither of them seemed to be employed. "Oh yes, I told them, I'd love to hear about what you do!"

They smiled, and one of them said, "We are aliens from another planet and we inhabit human bodies so we can mingle with the people on earth. In fact we rented this particular home because with it being more or less round, it reminds us of a spaceship.. The mother-ship is hovering just out of sight, and any time they call us we have to leave what we are doing and go home immediately."

I kind of blinked, were these ladies joking with me? I'd heard of aliens but I never pictured myself in a situation like this. And obviously their jobs were something I couldn't do. "But I've always been a fan of science fiction and I asked questions and was interested in all they had to say. So I asked them what sort of things they had to do to please their bosses on the mother ship."

They told us when they would go in a grocery store some people could sense that they were different and they would turn around in the middle of an aisle and go in the other direction but others didn't seem to notice we have different vibrations and they would smile at us and be friendly. Dogs seem to sense we are alien, but most people can't tell. They even went so far as to tell us they could buy furniture but were not allowed to buy a house. They did have a car and when they were called to leave they would just disappear, leaving their furniture behind.

In the long run their main job was to analyze the earthlings and give the information to the mothership. In many ways they told us the people on earth act and react much as they do, but they are trying to go deeper into the earthling's emotions. They even said we have some emotions they don't possess; but on the other hand the aliens have emotions that we do not possess."

"It was a bit strange living next to them, but they were friendly to us, and when we made visits to Las Vegas, they would gather our mail out of the mailbox, and if we called them before heading back to Sedona they would go in our house and turn on the heat or the A/C, depending on the season. We had entrusted them with a key to our house. They are gone now, but it was fascinating listening to their stories."

"Wow" Smitty said, "I've never heard of anything like that in my entire life! Does any one else know anything that was strange or out-of-the-ordinary?" One man on the edge of the group laughed, and said, "This is not about aliens or stuff, but we have our own cross-dresser here in Sedona. He walks up and down Highway 89 all day long and all he does is wave at each and every car. I think he's homeless, but he's always clean and friendly, and I know he doesn't work anywhere."

Ragetti grinned, "We haven't had the pleasure of seeing him/her as yet. Have any of you been to the vortexes and had anything unusual happen?"

"I'm Patty, and at the vortex that is on the way up to the airport, I checked it out; and no one was there at the time, so I just sat down, closed my eyes and relaxed. A great sense of peace came over me, something different than I've felt anywhere else. Sedona is a magical place to be."

"Thanks, folks, I've loved the stuff you've told us, so take a few of our cards and pass them around. Give us a call if you hear anything really bizarre, OK? We've got to get some rest, so goodnight all."

Everyone said goodnight as they went out the door, and Smitty noticed a sign on the door stating their hours were from eleven a.m. to eleven p.m. so they were almost ready to close.

"Are we actually going back to the motel? I've noticed the hours around here and they seem to roll up the sidewalks at five o'clock; all but the restaurants, of course. Evenings are a gold mine for them." Smitty looked over at Ragetti.

"Yes, I do plan on laying down, but only for a nap. Sometime in the middle of the night I'd like to dress all in black and go out poking around a little. See if there are any bodies moving around during that time. Sedona does not really have much in the way of entertainment at night."

"Good thing I brought black clothes" Smitty echoed. "I hope we don't get stranded up on some mountain and have to call in a rescue party."

Each of them changed into entirely black clothing and as they got to their car and pulled out of the well-lighted parking area, they realized just how dark it gets in Sedona. The town had a few streetlights; but the residential areas had none. It gave the words 'pitch black' new meaning.

"Do you have any idea where we are going?" Smitty asked Ragetti.

"I thought we'd drive toward the Village of Oak Creek, it seems like a very popular hike is up Courthouse Rock. Of course they are always rescuing someone from there also, but I'm trying not to think about that. We won't actually be climbing it; I just want to nose around and see if any living creatures are out in the middle of the night." Ragetti told Smitty.

"Why are you parking in front of the hardware store" Smitty looked bewildered.

"It's as inconspicuous as any where, I really don't think the cops around here are wasting a lot of time checking out parked cars this time of night. They are probably sleeping."

"Which is exactly what I'd like to be doing," Smitty grumbled. But both of them got out of the car and walked a couple of blocks to get to the entrance to the trail marked 'Courthouse Rock.'

Smitty for one had no desire to climb up the side of a rock this steep; because everyone knew going down was even harder than going up. Even when he had come to Sedona with his family he had never tried to climb Courthouse Rock. You read in the papers all the time about how some person got stranded up there and had to be rescued by helicopter.

"Get out your small flashlight, we'll be able to see where our next step is, but it should not be visible to anyone looking up at the rock. And there isn't much of a moon tonight, so we are quite inconspicuous."

Ragetti by this time was about five or six feet in front of Smitty, and while he was not anxious to be rock climbing with it pitch black outside, Ragetti had to look at ease or he'd never get Smitty to follow him.

"Smitty said, "Just a minute, I have to tie my shoe." As he bent down a bullet went whizzing over the top of his head.

Ragetti had his gun out and took a shot at a dark image about thirty feet in front of them. He thought he heard someone cuss, and there was a rustling through the bushes, then complete silence. "I think I hit someone. But as we don't know the trail it's not a good time to check and see if we can spot any blood. We'll have to come back in the morning and check this out further."

"Oh, thank God," Smitty shuttered. "If I hadn't had to tie my shoe just then I'd be laying here dead."

"We don't know that for sure, Smitty, but Thank the Lord you did bend over just then to tie your shoe. And I'm sure we winged him, we're coming back up here early in the morning and see if we can spot any blood up ahead on the trail."

"And I suppose you want to get up here before anyone else has a chance to trample through the evidence, knowing you," Smitty sighed.

"Right again, and just in case someone may like to get up ridiculously early to start their hike, I'm calling the Parks Department and asking them to close this trailhead until further notice so we won't have to worry about our evidence," Ragetti smiled at Smitty and said, "see if we have time to get two or three more hours of sleep."

"Hell, I'm so tired and frustrated right now I feel like I could sleep for two days straight and maybe never go hiking again," Smitty grumbled.

The next morning the two agents got up and Ragetti appeased Smitty in a small way by telling him there was no hurry to get to the trailhead, the Park Service assured them it would be closed and they would keep an eye on it – let's go have a huge breakfast wherever you want."

Smitty looked at him suspiciously, "You know I don't know any of the restaurants in this town, so you just threw that in to make me feel good."

Ragetti laughed and said, "You got it partner! Let's just make the best of this spooky little town, maybe we'll have it solved in a couple of days."

The two agents ate a hearty breakfast, and had to admit it was one of the better meals they had eaten lately. From there they made their way from Poco Diablo where they had eaten on down 179 until they came to the entrance of Courthouse Rock. True to their word, the parking lot had a yellow tape across it, and the trailhead itself was posted with a "no admission" sign.

One Park Ranger was standing by, and foregoing the aliases they both had, they pulled out their badges and told the Ranger exactly who they were. They let it be known they were in town undercover as journalists. The Park Rangers had not been informed of the seriousness of what was happening in their quiet little town, and they offered to guide the two agents up the path to the point they had thought they had winged the assailant. And their help was much appreciated as Smitty and Ragetti had not done much hiking lately. As they moved slowly up the hill, one of the Park Rangers who had very sharp eyes, said it looked like a fresh bullet had just struck the guava that rose beside the trail. Smitty looked around and said he though this was just about the spot where he had decided to tie his shoe.

"It always helps to have a bullet from the gun that was shooting at you" the ranger said as he took a knife and dug it out of the soft guava. Slipping it into a little evidence bag he handed it over to Agent Ragetti.

"You've been a bigger help than you can imagine. I don't suppose there is anywhere close by where they can study this bullet and find out the type and gun that was used. Do we have to take this all the way down to the Phoenix area to be analyzed?"

The older ranger spoke up and said, "We seldom have anything like this come up, but one way you could save time is to send it with the Super Shuttle. It would save the two of you a lot of time, or you could check with FedEx and see if they would do it." He shrugged his shoulders.

Chapter Seven

AS THEY MADE THEIR way further up the hill they both felt hopeful that something would come of all this. Having a bullet proved there was a shot fired at them. Now if they could just find some blood on the trail, proving the shooter had been hit they would finally have a clue to work with.

"How do you guys put up with all the weird shit that goes on in this town? All the crazy things people believe in? What made them choose Sedona instead of one of the other towns?"

Ragetti looked around and saw the beautiful scenery, but even though it extended to just this one small town, there had to be a scientific reason.

"I think it's because of the vortexes located in the area. And people love to gossip. I've heard of more weird stories and people since being stationed here than I have in my entire life. And most of the working people don't actually live in Sedona; real estate here is out of sight so most of us live in Cornville or Cottonwood. Believe me, it's a lot more normal there."

Ragetti stopped and looked around as he said, "We should be reaching the spot in the trail where I saw the shadow; it seemed like there was a rock hanging out over the trail, and that's where the shadow was."

"Yes, there is a spot just like you described just ahead in fact; that looks like blood splatter on the rock just ahead."

Ragetti and Smitty hurried ahead, anxious to see what this mysterious being had done after being hit. The brush on the right side of the trail was trampled as they stepped off the trail and they could see a pool of blood as the shooter had obviously stopped to try and put a tourniquet around his leg or thigh to stop the flow of blood.

"Let's follow the path down that he took – it shouldn't be too hard, after all he was wounded." The rangers had an easy time following his trail, and Smitty and Ragetti were happy to just trail along behind them. Eventually they came out a short distance from where the parking space was. There were distinct tire tread and they could see he had wasted no time getting out of the area.

Ragetti was busy taking photos of the cars tire tracks. "At least we can send this to our researcher using our cellphone, too bad we couldn't do the same with the bullet. I also want to get a sample of that blood pool we found; it's definitely plenty for DNA."

One of the rangers spoke up, "I don't know if this will help or not, but being the shooter was here in the Village of Oak Creek, it could be he lived in one of the more exclusive homes you find along this route. There is a gated community about half way from the Village and the corner of 179 and 89A. Once we get information on the car we could easily find out who it is registered to and where they live."

Ragetto looked at Smitty and said, "I'm driving down to our lab. We have enough stuff to make the trip worthwhile, so we can get immediate answers. You can stay here, catch up on your sleep a little, and gather more folk-lore stories from people you encounter. That's your forte' so you'll get better results than I would. I'll be back this afternoon."

Smitty got in the car with Ragetti and was dropped off at the motel. He would have liked to be going to the Phoenix area, but Ragetti was right, one of them should stay here and go on with the interviews and observations. And of course Ragetti would be back this afternoon; so it wasn't like he was being abandoned by his partner. It just spooked him a little to know that he was alone. But Smitty would be close to their motel, and he knew he damn sure would not be doing any hiking alone. More interviews with tourists would be good, and there was a positive side to this also; since he and Ragetti had been in town there had been no further reports of people coming up missing.

Perhaps if the man Ragetti took a shot at was the one behind all of this, he would find it hard to kidnap people if he had been injured. And by the looks of that pool of blood Smitty figured the injury would have to be quite serious.

Smitty missed the idea of going to Phoenix with Ragetti, he may have had the chance to see his wife and boys; but they were on the clock and that's how it happened sometimes.

Patty was surprised to see Agent Ragetti when he pulled up to the office well before lunch. "Look who the early bird is; what did you do get up at five this morning?"

Ragetti gave Patty a hug, and laughing said to her, "you're right on target for when we got up, but we're gathering some clues. Smitty had someone take a shot at him, but luckily at that exact moment he had bent down to tie his shoe, so he's fine. I fired off a shot but it was still too dark to see anything; but we're quite sure I hit someone or something. All this happened last night and we got up early to check it out, that's why I need all these things done now or sooner."

"Well, the lab hasn't seen you for a few days, so maybe being you are working out of town, they will get right on it. Will you wait for the results?" Patty asked.

"No, I'll head back up to Sedona before this maniac gets a chance to add someone else to the list of missing persons. I know one thing; we're dealing with a whacko, probably one with more money than he knows what to do with it, and he is definitely dangerous. By the way, it's probably better if you don't mention the shooting to Victoria or Susan. We're both safe and that is all that really matters. See you soon, kiddo, take care."

And Ragetti left. It was very close to lunch time and he decided he had to eat somewhere, so why not go to The Shack – he knew the food was good there and it was right on the way. Besides that, Donna, the waitress, never asked questions.

Donna smiled when she caught sight of Ragetti. "It's been a long time since you've been in; what have you been doing, sleeping in?" Always in the mood to tease she gave Ragetti her biggest smile.

"Sweetheart, I've missed you too. Ya, I thought I'd skip town until the big scandal about the Pope being shot blew over in that particular case.

In that particular case whether you were the good guy or the bad guy the public will still hate you."

"Got it" Donna answered, "But according to the papers you're much more of a good guy than a bad guy. But I know what you mean; people just don't like to hear bad news. Are you planning on eating lunch or did you just stop by to talk?"

"I'll take a grilled cheese sandwich and a bowl of chili then I've got to head out of town again. Oh, and a cup of coffee while I'm waiting please."

As Ragetti sat waiting for his lunch he had an urge to call Smitty's wife, Susan. He had his hand on the phone, but decided it was best for her to hear about the shooting later, probably much, much later, if at all.

Here was Donna with his coffee and his chili. "Your grilled cheese sandwich will be right out." It was a busy day so she left with no further chit-chat.

Ragetti sat and pondered how differently things could have turned out. He hated to admit to himself how close a friend Smitty had become. Losing him would be like losing half of himself so he tried to turn his thoughts in other directions. As soon as he heard from the lab he had a feeling things would fall into place quite fast, the tires could give him a clue to the car, the car would show the owner, address and all. Then it was just a matter of getting to him and arresting him. He decided he would not give the Sedona Police the danger of driving down to FBI Headquarters in Phoenix. To them it would seem like an exciting part of their job, but if anything happened to them with that maniac, he would never forgive himself. Then they would be free to see their families again, and be back to their normal life.

Laughing at himself, he thought, "but this IS our normal life." Taking a last sip of his coffee he left Donna a good tip and stopped by to settle the bill. The drive to Sedona seemed long and boring. He wondered if his partner had caught up on his sleep, and if he had discovered any new information. The minute Ragetti made it to Sedona, he headed straight for the motel; but the room was empty. Grabbing his cell he called Smitty.

"Smitty here, are you back in the beautiful Red Rock Country?" came the smart reply.

"Yes, I'm back, couldn't stay away another minute, so where are you?" Ragetti asked.

"Sitting in the shade enjoying an iced coffee – come on over and join me and we'll catch up on things. I'm at the open-air restaurant just up the street."

"I'll be right over" was Ragetti's reply and out the door he went. He thought about walking over to the restaurant overlooking uptown, but then if they needed to leave quickly they wouldn't have a car, so he ended up driving. As he sat down a waiter came over and Ragetti said, "I'll have an iced coffee also." Then he sat down and filled Smitty in on his quick trip.

"The lab said they would get right on it, and they were going to send the results to Patty as well as texting me. So we should hear something quite soon. I'll tell you it was very tempting, but the only person I spoke to was Patty, and I told her to keep my quick trip between the two of us. How's it going with you?"

Smitty took a deep breath as he began his story. "My cellphone rang this morning and it was a local number and one I didn't recognize so I answered 'David Erickson' how can I help you?" The voice on the other end was a male, sounded middle-aged and told me his name was Henry Halvorson, and he had heard there were a couple of journalists in town seeking out stories about the vortexes or any other strange happenings that you don't find in other towns. His son was evidently in the group we talked to the night we were eating Mexican food and he had passed the information on to his father. Rumors carry fast in a town like this, and it wouldn't surprise me if half the town doesn't already know about us."

Ragetti: "What sort of news or story did Mr. Halvorson have for you?"

"He said he lives on 179, across from Poco Diablo Country Club and many times he is unable to sleep late at night. Usually as he looks out at his neighborhood all the houses are dark, but he said once or twice a week he noticed this one house with several lights on. He could not tell exactly which house it was, but it seemed to be shortly before the entrance gate to the Chapel of the Holy Cross. He has even driven over there during the daytime to see if he could ascertain exactly which house it was."

Ragetti: "Has he seen any people or cars around the house?"

"Although it was some distance away he said it looked like car lights driving up to the house when the house was lighted up late at night. The lights would stay on for maybe an hour or so after the arrival of the car, then it would all go dark like the other homes."

Just then Ragetti's cellphone rang and he saw it was Patty. "Hey good lookin', you have some news for me already?"

Patty: "The lab said the tire treads are from a large Lincoln or Cadillac, but they could not come up with anything more specific as yet. However on the DNA of the blood sample, we hit pay dirt. It belongs to Richard L. Peters, former doctor. I did a quick background check on him and it seems he had a very lucrative practice in Phoenix until about five years ago. Although he was only sixty years old, he decided to retire and move to Sedona. He has written a number of small booklets on Sedona describing the vortexes, and elaborating that even now there may be many of the local residents who are aliens. He's a well-educated man, but has really gotten caught up in all this woo-woo stuff of Sedona. He is single, losing his wife shortly before he retired, so he has been immersing himself in the local clubs, etc. who believe whole-heartedly that there is alien life and that many are of them are already in Sedona."

Ragetti: "What do you have listed as his address?"

"That would be 2010 White Heron Drive, Sedona, AZ. I'm trying to come up with a photo from his DNA, but so far no luck. I did see an article on him describing him as tall, athletic, salt and pepper hair and nice looking. Being he was a surgeon he has a doctorate degree, and I believe he was educated at Harvard. I haven't checked into his bank accounts as yet, but he does own other property other than the house in Sedona. I'll give you more as I get it. Bye for now."

Smitty said, "What are we waiting for, let's get in the car and see just where 2010 White Heron Drive is located. Maybe if we're lucky we'll see a Lincoln or a Cadillac parked out front."

Both jumped up and headed for their car, eager to see where the shooter may actually live and wondering how they could gather enough proof to get a search warrant for his home.

Ragetti entered the address into the GPS, but as it began giving them the directions on where to turn they found they were not headed down 179 at all, but rather uptown into some of the newer settlements higher up into the hills. As they were driving, continually getting higher and higher they were amazed at the solitude and beauty of Sedona. This is what realtors were talking about when they said tourists come to Sedona and get "Red Rock Fever." It was as if God had stretched out his hand and in his hand he held the beauty and red rocks of Sedona, so unlike the countryside outside the relatively small area of Sedona. It was not hard to imagine Sedona as a magical place and an oasis like this always attracted all sorts of people. Those who could afford the high price of living in Sedona lived in the lap of luxury. For those folks who could barely afford the prices in the restaurants, much less buying a house, they became the forest people and other labels that had been stuck on them. As they drove along they could see this is where some of the big money houses were. Views galore and yet still a sense of privacy that you never see in most cities. They finally came to a left hand turn that had a sign stating this was a private driveway, and although it did not have an electric gate; Ragetti doubted that most locals or tourists would not venture up the driveway unless it was by invitation. But of course, looking private and exclusive had never bothered them before, so Ragetti turned up the driveway and wound his way around a couple of corners until they were faced with a massive two-story home, all made of brick, but with a very modern design. The windows were huge and the view seemed to go forever, without another house in sight anywhere.

Ragetti stopped the car at the bottom of some artistically layered round steps, and proceeded to approach the front door. He had a feeling the owner knew they were approaching the minute they had turned up the driveway. He had the address in his hand on a small piece of paper, and as the door opened, he asked "Is this the residence of Tom Henry? As you can see it is the one given to me, but I certainly was not expecting anything as grand as this."

The man was tall, athletic and had salt and pepper hair; he was also supporting himself with a cane. He looked at Ragetti and recognized a professional, regardless of the clothing. He had studied people far too long to be fooled by the clothing they wore. "You certainly do have the right address, but this home is not the residence of Tom Henry. In fact, I don't believe any of my close neighbors have that name."

Ragetti had the feeling the man could read his every thought, it made him uncomfortable, but he smiled and said, "I'm sorry to have bothered you, especially now that I see you have hurt your leg, it must be very painful to try and move around. I hope you have someone to care for you."

The homeowner looked at him and smiled, "Thank you, but don't worry about me, I have many people come by to help me out. I hope you find the right address for your friend. I would suggest stopping by the Post Office, they can be very helpful."

Ragetti thanked him again and walked back to the car. He motioned for Smitty to remain quiet as he had the creepy feeling that every move was being recorded and perhaps even any words they may say to one another.

Once they reached a couple of miles away from the house Ragetti began to talk. "I know this is being paranoid and maybe I'm letting some of the old folk lore tales get to me, but that man I'm positive is our shooter. His leg was all bandaged up and he walked with the assistance of a cane. It's like he was looking right into my mind and reading every thought in my head. Burr! I would hate to meet up with him on a dark trail, he reeks of evil."

Smitty couldn't believe his ears, hearing Ragetti talk like this was a first time ever, and if he felt like that; just hearing his talk made Smitty get goosebumps up and down his arms. "Other than the obvious fact that the damage to his leg could well have been when you shot at that shadow the other night; anything else that didn't add up?"

"No, of course I couldn't see inside his house, the small glimpse I did get looked normal enough, it was all just the feeling I got the moment he opened the door," Ragetti replied.

"I'm heading back to the motel; I could use a good cup of coffee. Yeah, I'm spooked and I don't like the feeling at all. I swear to God it was like meeting up with Satin himself! Not only that; but the man fits the description the woman over in the Village of Oak Creek gave us. The one who slipped on one of the trails and probably would have been dead if the man had not sat himself directly in her path; so she hit him instead of plunging over the edge."

Smitty looked at him in amazement and said, "Maybe you need something a little stronger than coffee."

Pulling into the motel parking lot, as soon as they got to their room Ragetti grabbed a beer from the refrigerator and plopped down on his bed. "First thing I'm going to do is call the lab and see if they have come up with anything more specific, then we'll talk to Patty, because if they informed her of anything she probably already knows the guys bank account and anything else there is to know about him."

Smitty decided to make a pot of coffee and eat a sandwich. He made two as Ragetti was never aware of hunger; his thoughts were entirely on the case. Sometimes Smitty though how handy it would be if he could be like that himself. He had no idea how a person could keep their mind off food. Everywhere you looked food was displayed, especially on TV. Having his domestic chores done he sat the two plates down on a little table, and as soon as the coffee was done he poured a cup for himself. He listened to the one-sided conversation Ragetti was having on the phone.. After hearing a few comments like "You don't say" or "No kidding" plus "And how much time did he spend doing that?" he gave up trying to figure it out and concentrated on enjoying his sandwich and coffee.

Ragetti finally finished the call, and immediately dialed Patty. Now the comments on Ragetti's end were even more vague than the other call had been. "Good girl; that's great; did you send the information to us already; and I think we might be nearly ready for a search warrant." After they hung up he looked and Smitty and said, "Is that extra sandwich for me?" Then he sat down, got up again to pour coffee, and started to eat. Smitty didn't say a word; he knew Ragetti well enough to know he had learned a lot on his phone call, so he let him eat and just sat sipping on his coffee until his partner was ready to talk.

Ragetti got up and started walking back and forth across the room. He always did his best thinking when he was on the move. "They narrowed the car down to a Navigator, so with Patty having that information, she began a methodical check of people in Sedona, including the Village of Oak Creek, to see how many were registered here. Of course most people own other property, and it could well be registered in a different county or even a different state. The fact that Sedona is split between two different counties (Yavapai and Coconino) doesn't make the job easier. One pays taxes to Prescott, and the other to Flagstaff. But she was lucky enough to find on the Coconino side a Navigator registered to Richard L. Peters, which is the house we just visited.

What he was doing at three a.m. over in the Village of Oak Creek is beyond me; but I think it's the same man that we encountered on the trail. At that time he didn't have the injured leg that occurred after he encountered us. She also checked out his bank account. Locally he keeps about a million dollars right in Sedona, and several other bank accounts are scattered around the country, probably some foreign accounts too.

With all that information she is sure the local police or the sheriff's department will issue us a search warrant. I don't know what we can expect to find in his house – dead bodies, the rest of the missing woman, I just don't know."

"I for one," Ragetti continued, "think we're dealing with a person who definitely is not your average human being; and I think we should have reinforcements with us when we go in with the search warrant. Just looking at the guy makes me feel like shooting him; but if we take along enough other people maybe we'll be lucky enough to have one of them get the drop on him and we'll be able to transport him back to FBI Headquarters."

"I'm going to take a short rest, and then we'll go speak with the sheriff. If we're going to do the search warrant thing it should be during the day while there is still plenty of light. I have a feeling this guy is a night owl, so I'd prefer having him home when we search his house."

"I think a nap is a good idea," Smitty joined in, "I feel a little shook up myself, just looking at you."

It was about three p.m. when they pulled into the sheriff station and they saw Sheriff Bauer's car out front, so hopefully he was in the office. As the two agents entered the small building they saw Sheriff Bauer seated at a desk inside a glassed in office. He immediately motioned them in. So in they went, and all of them settled around a small conference table.

The Sheriff started right out without pulling any punches "What have you guys been up to? I've got a gut feeling that you've come up with some further clues as to what happened to the missing people, and maybe even the dead woman." The Sheriff had a feeling these guys didn't miss too much, and he was really glad they were here to help solve this.

Ragetti decided to lay it all out to the Sheriff from the beginning and see what his take on this would be. "We arrived here posing as journalists so tourists and locals alike would be eager to tell us their stories. And we did hear some really weird stuff, but nothing that would give us a clue. There was one man, a Henry Halvorson who lives somewhere off 179 and he was suspicious of one of his neighbors. He couldn't pin point the exact house, but he said it was either in a gated community over by the Chapel of the Holy Cross or in the vicinity. There were several different evenings, well into the middle of the night; where he would see this house all lit up and once he saw a car approach and obviously pulled into the garage. He would watch and after about an hour or so had passed, all the lights went out and it was again pitch black."

Ragetti stood up, but continued to talk, "I drove down with our little supply of evidence to the lab that takes care of our department in the West Valley of Phoenix and also checked in with our researcher to see if she had anything new. I lucked out with the lab as they have narrowed down the search to a Navigator. Of course the hard part there is that we've got two counties just in this one little town, and for many this is just a part-time residence, so the car or SUV could easily be registered in another state. But Patty found one Navigator registered to a Mr. Richard L. Peters and his address was listed as 2010 White Heron Drive. Patty also gave us a vague description of Mr. Peters but thus far hasn't come up with a photo.

He is a retired doctor, and needless to say he has more money than God; placed in various accounts, including a million he keeps right here in Sedona."

The Sheriff looked at Ragetti in astonishment, "I can't believe you've found out all this in an amazingly short period of time." He looked at Ragetti with admiration.

Ragetti stopped to grab a cup of coffee before he started to go on with his findings. "When Smitty and I drove up to 2010 White Heron Drive I was expecting our GPS to take us over toward the Village of Oak Creek. Instead it took us through uptown and far up into the rocks and scenic areas with homes snuggled into little areas so you hardly noticed they were there. It must have been a real challenge to build the damn things."

"So after travelling five or maybe eight miles we come to this driveway marked "Private Drive" – no gate or anything but from the time we took that turn until we arrived at the house we had the feeling that eyes were on us.

The house itself was a marvel of architecture, and as I went to ring the doorbell it took awhile before someone came to the door. When the door was finally opened I was not surprised to see a professional looking man, very much like Patty had described him to be. The best part is that one leg was all bandaged up; probably in what's called a splint or cast. I did not ask him his name but instead asked if this was the home of Tom Henry and showed him the address I had on a small piece of paper.

He didn't offer his name, but said he couldn't recall any of his neighbors by the name of Tom Henry. At that point I mentioned it must be very painful to navigate with his sore leg and I hoped he had someone to help care for him.

He thanked me and said, 'don't worry about me; I have many people stopping by.' And at that point there was nothing more to do than leave."

The Sheriff let out a deep breath. "And you think this guy is the shooter and could be the person behind the missing people and the woman who is supposedly dead?"

"Yes! It's only a gut feeling, but he fits the evidence we found, and it was his DNA in that pool of blood where he shot and narrowly missed hitting Smitty and it proved the shot I got off hit it's mark."

"What do you want to do next?" the Sheriff asked.

"I think we have enough for a search warrant of his property, but I want more than just Smitty and I to go there, I think we should have several reinforcements as it's a big place and we have no idea what we're going to find. It could be very dangerous. Also it should be done during the daylight as we know the shooter is a night person. I'd hate to see another person killed or come up missing tonight."

"Did you bring vests with you and uniforms, or do you need to borrow some?" the Sheriff asked.

"Oh we're all set in that department; we just need you to supply about eight men. I want to look as menacing as possible to deter Mr. Peters and possibly others who may be inside the house. The more people we have the less resistance we'll get."

"We can be ready in about fifteen minutes. Go to your motel and change clothes, we will take you in our cars, so you and Smitty can both ride with me. We will pick you up shortly at your motel. Maybe you can come out front when you're ready."

The Sheriff grinned at them. "Having you guys in town has really added to the excitement, hell we haven't had this much fun in years. It's seldom that anything of any consequence happens here."

The agents said goodbye and drove back to their motel.

"My God," Smitty said, "they act like this whole thing is exciting and fun. You can tell they don't deal with killers very often. They don't seem to realize how dangerous this could be."

"That's what happens when you get assigned to a small town. It's dull but much safer than what we have to go through," was Ragetti's curt reply.

Ragetti and Smitty hurriedly changed into their life vests and uniforms; then they hurried out to the front of the motel where they could slip quickly into the Sheriff's car when he came by. They got some curious stares to see two FBI Special Agents standing on the corner, but no one dared stop and ask what they were doing in Sedona. People are not usually too anxious to speak with FBI agents.

Sheriff Bauer pulled up followed by about five police cars. It looked like they had gathered up everyone they had. The agents jumped in and they were on their way. Of course the Sheriff did not have to use his GPS, he turned on his siren and flashing lights and the traffic came to a dead stop. This was an unusual sight for Sedona, and for a few minutes all the tourists stopped and stared as they sped through uptown. As they proceeded toward White Huron Drive, the Sheriff cut his siren and turned off the flashing lights. Ragetti noticed all the police cars behind them followed suit.

"Uptown is always such a mess, and with so many tourists running here and there I figured it was the easiest and safest way to get through town," Sheriff Bauer told them.

It wasn't long before they were at the private drive leading to Mr. Peter's home, and at that time everyone grew a lot more serious. They knew Mr. Peters would be aware of their arrival, but with his bad leg they didn't think he would try to run. The police and sheriff swarmed into all space in front of the house. No one would be able to enter nor could they leave.

Ragetti and the Sheriff walked to the front door; rang the doorbell after announcing "FBI, Open the Door!"

Mr. Peters was calm and collected as he came to the door. He smiled and said, "Have you come to collect a donation for new uniforms. Just one person would do as I would be happy to donate to your cause." He gave them a charming smile.

Ragetti handed him the search warrant and said "I am Special Agent Ragetti with the FBI and we have a valid search warrant to go through your property. We will be careful not to destroy anything of value, and we would like you to sit down on the sofa with one of the officers and stay out of our way, but do not leave."

The smile wiped itself off Mr. Peters face and he knew it was useless to argue with them, so he may as well sit down and wait it out. The various officers spread through the downstairs and about four of them headed up to the bedroom area.

Ragetti tried the door that probably led to a basement and found it locked. "Do you wish to give me the key to this door, Mr. Peters, or would you prefer we break it down?"

Mr. Peters immediately reached into his pocket and handed the key over to the officer who was sitting with him. Then it was handed over to Ragetti.

Ragetti looked around and saw Smitty enter the room. "Hey Smitty, come with me to check out the basement." As they walked down a steep stairway they could smell a peculiar odor in the air that was different from the rest of the house.

Chapter Eight

"WHAT KIND OF SMELL is that, it's awful, but it's not one I can identify?" Smitty said as he rubbed at his nose.

Ragetti saw the light switch and the basement was flooded with light. "I'm almost afraid to tell you what that smell reminds me of, but I can tell you one thing; before we leave this room we'll know what happened to the missing people."

The basement had been set up efficiently to serve as an operating room and there was also an electronic garage door making it convenient to drive right into the basement from the back of the house. There was an area in the far corner that had been partitioned off, and the door was closed. The closer they moved toward it the stronger the smell became.

"I don't think I'm going to like this part," Smitty said, and he already looked slightly sick to his stomach.

"Come on, partner, don't think of it that way --- this is the pot of gold at the end of the rainbow. Take a deep breath and it might help to hold your hanky in front of your nose. OK, here we go!" And Ragetti stepped through the door.

They both stopped in shock, for the room was basically build like a spa, except the liquid in the huge tub type of device taking up most of the room definitely was not filled with water. As Ragetti moved closer to the tub he realized he was looking at muriatic acid. That explained why no evidence was ever found on any of the missing bodies. One day in this solution and there would not be as much left of a person than if they had been cremated.

Ragetti's stomach rolled as he imagined all the people that had been thrown into this tub filled with acid, probably while they were still alive. It was beyond horrible and he was sure he would never get this sight and smell out of his brain – never!

Smitty could not handle it at all, and he had found a small bathroom where he was busy vomiting. He had never in his entire life encountered anything or anyone so evil. He doubted he would ever want to come to Sedona again, regardless of how beautiful it was.

Ragetti went to the stairway and yelled to the Sheriff, "Come on down in the basement and bring a couple of guys with you as witnesses." Then he began to search around for evidence of whom or what may have been given an acid bath. Obviously they were not going to have a body. As he opened a cabinet door he found stacks of backpacks, purses, and even a few pictures belonging to the people he had murdered.

As the Sheriff and three of policemen came down it didn't take long before one or two of them found their way to the bathroom also. For some of them it could have been the first time they had encountered the stench of death. In fact one policeman looked around, taking in what had happened and ran for the stairs yelling "Oh My God!"

They came upstairs and Smitty stepped up to Mr. Peters, told him to stand, and cuffed him as he was reading him his rights. Peters looked at them in shock, "How can you arrest me, you have found nothing that proves a crime was ever committed. I'll sue you for this type of treatment and you'll never work as an agent again."

Ragetti said, "I'm calling FBI Headquarters and ask them to send two agents up to get Peters, some vehicle where he can be locked in the back and won't be able to touch either of the agents. He's dangerous and one never knows what he may do next. I don't want to expose any of the police here to a maniac like this. Have someone watch him at all times until the FBI arrives to pick him up. I want to make sure this madman doesn't have a chance to touch anyone."

He turned to the Sheriff and said, "Let's get back to town, if I hurry I can be in time to see my family for a late dinner."

As they drove back toward uptown Sedona there was very little conversation. Everyone seemed lost in their own private thoughts. Smitty was thinking that here was a man who had been a successful businessman; and what could have happened that had turned his life into this lifestyle that was nothing except evil? He had all the money in the world. What had made him listen to these weirdos he was associating with and spending his time with? What caused him to snap, and yet still appear so normal?

Ragetti tried hard to clear his mind of the smells and sights he had just left. He tried to imagine how excited Victoria would be to see him home again. He thought he would wait until tomorrow to meet with Brown because it was all too vivid and fresh in his mind right now. He just wanted the familiarity of home. Seeing Victoria would help clear the images out of his mind, and right now that's all he wanted to think about.

The Sheriff also was quiet as he analyzed all that had happened. What could cause a man living in Sedona to go crazy, killing people like he was the star of a fantasy movie and was the most evil being on earth, killing, torturing and who knows what else? It made him feel somewhat paranoid to be in the position he was in. Would there be other monsters coming out of the wood work, sneaking around in the mysterious beauty of the town, waiting to create evil actions? He wondered if it might be time to consider retirement, he never wanted to go through something like this again.

As they reached the motel, their goodbyes were rather short, each person knowing that it was hard to react like a normal person after what they had seen and although what they had not seen was even worse, it was still something they wanted out of their minds.

Ragetti said he was going to haul their stuff to the car and change into a pair of jeans and a tee-shirt. He told Smitty if he had time perhaps he could notify the office that they were checking out. Smitty nodded and began putting his stuff together.

Ragetti used his phone to text Victoria, all his message said was 'hold dinner for me tonight.' He then called Sheriff Bauer and told him the FBI Special Agents should be arriving to pick up Richard Peters within a hour or two as they were already on their way. I'd suggest you put him somewhere that he won't be seen by anyone entering the jail. You never know how many crazy friends he may have in this town. Better to be safe than sorry.

All their stuff was loaded in the car and as they climbed in Ragetti slapped the steering wheel and said, "Dammit! We should have picked up some kind of souvenir for Patty. It's not like she expects things like that, but she deserves to be treated special."

Smitty laughed, "Ragetti, you're getting soft now that you're happily married. I think some of my good traits are starting to rub off on you. But don't worry, I thought of it and I've taken care of it already. What did you think I was doing when you left me alone at the motel, just sitting around watching TV?"

Ragetti reached out and punched him on the shoulder; he should know his partner well enough by now to know he never missed a detail. As they drove through the Village of Oak Creek on their way to Hwy. 17 both of them were unusually silent.

Finally Smitty broke the silence. "You know, my wife and I have been up here with the boys a couple of times. The restaurants were a little above our spending level, so we mostly camped out and spent a lot of time at Slide Rock. I never thought much about the weird people we would see, cross-dressers and all the talk about vortexes. To me it was just a small, quiet little town that I figured would be incredibly dull to actually live in. But it was a fun and exciting place to come even though it was way above our scale. I never thought I would be coming here on an assignment and see some of the stuff that can go on. The rich people in the big houses don't deserve to be placed above us. It's just like every other race, religion, or whatever you want to compare. There are bad apples in every barrel."

Ragetti looked at him and said, "I know you've been up here more than I have. I can imagine that at some point in our lives Victoria and I will drive up and spend the week-end here, look at the shops and eat in some fancy restaurant. But I will always have this other view of Sedona stuck in my head. It's beautiful, but I thank the Lord; it's way above my budget."

"I'll be happy to have Brown call us and tell us to come right over to his office, and we'll head over there to find out what our next case will be. The last two have been pretty strange, so it will be nice to get back to some murders or drug crimes,"

Smitty laughed to himself. Ragetti looked at Smitty and knew this eerie stuff would still go on for a week or so, there was the questioning of Richard Peters; that would be enough to make anyone's skin crawl. He wondered vaguely if the man would even be declared competent to stand trial. Smitty reached out and turned on the radio. Soft music floated out, just the kind he was in the mood for. He wanted to phone Susan; but he just didn't have the energy. Instead he reclined his seat back slightly and closed his eyes. He must have fallen asleep for a bit because when he opened his eyes he saw they were almost at their exit to get off on Highway 101. And the clock said it was a little after six o'clock, so even as diligent as Brown was, he would have gone home by now. Thank God today was Thursday and they would only have to work one more day and it would be the week-end. He knew in his mind Friday would be full of facing Brown and Peters in interviews. But tonight he would see his wife and kids again, and life would be normal.

Ragetti had noticed that his partner had fallen asleep for close to an hour, but the trip had been so unnerving for both of them he decided to let him just sleep. He should have called Susan and told her he was on the way home. So it would be a big surprise for Susan when Smitty got home and just about in time for dinner too. Ragetti didn't know why he had decided not to surprise his own wife; but it would be fun; and knowing Victoria he didn't have to worry about her badgering him with a thousand questions. They saw most of the lights were off in many of their offices, so Ragetti told Smitty he was just going to check in quickly at the Main Office, just to make sure Peters had been processed. He said, "You look like hell, so wait until I check in to make sure Peters is here. You know, on second thought I'm going to just take you to your house, and I stop by here on my way home. It could be you'll be in time for dinner. Maybe you can enjoy your evening. We'll start on Peters as soon as we finish briefing Brown.

Smitty didn't have to think twice about the offer. He told Ragetti he would owe him one; and they backed out to head for Smitty's house.

As they pulled into Smitty's drive he grabbed his stuff and got it all transferred to his front porch with a little help from Ragetti. He was so happy to be away from Sedona and at his own home, he even smiled "Goodnight Partner, have a good evening." He said as he was about to enter his house.

As Smitty walked into the house the family was just sitting down to eat. Susan jumped up and gave him a big kiss. "I don't know why but I had a feeling you would be home tonight, so I cooked one of your favorites."

"That sounds like music to my ears. Come to think of it, I'm starving! Come here boys and give your old pop a hug. Believe it or not, I missed you." The boys came running over and soon the whole family stood in a huddle thankful to be back together again.

Ragetti headed over to the Main Office and going inside; went to the area where they do all the processing of newly arrested people. "I'm Agent Ragetti, can you tell me if the prisoner from Sedona, Richard L. Peters, has been processed?"

"Ya, we've got him – and boy is he a weirdo from the word go. I haven't heard all the details of what he's done, but it should be quite the story to hear his version of what he was up to." The officer shook his head and mumbled something about 'crazier than a loon.'

Ragetti pulled up to his house and was glad to see both Victoria's car and Patty's car in the garage. His heart did a little double beat as he thought of Victoria. It would be so damn good to be home again and holding her in his arms. As he stepped in through the kitchen door he heard squeals and giggles coming from the table as they both ran to hug him. He gave a hug to Patty and a long kiss to Victoria.

Then Victoria gave him a hit on the shoulder and said, "You might have called your new bride and let her know how things were going on the case! Just little details like 'I'm still alive' would have been nice. But lucky you, I will forgive you this time, and you're right in time for dinner." After several hugs and kisses he felt wide awake and the horror of the past few days seemed to have happened a long time ago.

"OMG!" Patty said, "I want to know every little detail about the Sedona incident. It may be a little kinky, but I've always loved going there – so I want to know everything!"

Victoria looked at her sister with daggers in her eyes. "Patty, the man has barely entered the door, he just captured the criminal and he has driven all the way from Sedona. Don't you think it might be a good idea to give him a night of peace and quiet?"

Patty immediately looked a little guilty, and smiling at Ragetti she said, "Well, I for one am starving, shall we all sit down for dinner?"

Victoria walked to the refrigerator and removed a bottle of beer for Ragetti, and against all rules she handed it to him right in the bottle. Patty looked at her sister and almost said, "Who are you, and what have you done with Victoria?" but although she thought it, she was smart enough to keep the thought to herself. They all gathered around the table and this time saying grace was more of a prayer, they all had so much to be thankful for and it felt so good to be a family again.

When the meal was completed, Victoria suggested that Ragetti grab a bottle of wine and she would get a couple of glasses and they would go to their room, have a drink and watch TV.

Patty took the cue and said she would be happy to clear the table and get things straightened up in the kitchen. She was reading a really good book and planned on going to bed early so she could finish it.

It didn't take Ragetti long to choose the wine and up the stairs they went. First thing for him was to get in a steaming hot shower, and he wasn't sure if even that would make him feel clean. This case had shaken him up more than he wanted to admit to himself. In fact, he felt so serious about it, he decided to it would be a good idea to stop by and see the shrink at work. The usual thing was the men usually had to be physically forced to talk to 'Doc Henry' but this is the first time he could ever remember actually looking forward to going. He made a mental note to himself to talk to Smitty about it; he had a feeling his partner was in even worse shape than him.

But he toweled himself off, and put it behind him for the evening. Pulling on a robe he found Victoria already cuddled up in the recliner for two that was easily his favorite chair in the house. The wine was poured; she gave him a sexy smile, and wiggled her finger at him, beckoning him to come and join her in the cuddling and drinking.

He knew that Victoria had to work the graveyard shift tonight, so a couple of glasses of wine and they would be going to bed also. He was actually so exhausted both mind and body that all he really wanted was to feel her soft body lying next to him. He very much doubted if he would even wake up when she was getting ready to go to work.

Victoria just chatted about various funny little things that had happened at the police station where she worked. She could tell Ragetti was worn out through and through, so she just wanted to be there for him, let him forget the case and settle down into a normal life again. It wasn't long before she suggested to him that maybe they should go to bed and get some sleep before she had to work all night. As they lay side by side she told him if he was able to sleep through the noise she made while getting ready for work, that she would understand if you have already left for work in the morning that she would understand not getting a goodbye kiss. And if you are gone before I get home I will understand that too. I'm just so happy to have you back home safe. And tomorrow is Friday; we have the entire week-end to do just as we please.

Ragetti barely had the energy left to mumble to her, "OK Sweetheart, good night."

Victoria could have lain awake for hours just looking at Ragetti she was so thrilled to have him home beside her, but always the practical one she closed her eyes and she too was soon in dreamland.

Chapter Nine

MORNING ROLLED AROUND MUCH too quickly, and Ragetti knew that when they got to the office they would report to Deputy Director Brown. He was surprised that he didn't even wake up when Victoria had gone to work, but he had really been worn out through and through. Seeing Deputy Director Brown would be the easy part. The next part was what they both dreaded, the interrogation of Richard L. Peters, maniac and evil to the core. It would not be a pleasant day for either of them.

He called Smitty and asked if he had eaten any breakfast as yet, and upon hearing that he had not, Ragetti suggested they meet at The Shack.

Donna greeted them with a big smile and a cup of coffee.

Ragetti laughed, and said, "Hey Sweetheart, could you put a little poison in my coffee today, I don't think I want to go to work?"

Donna stopped dead in her tracks, came around the counter and actually gave him a hug. Then she went back to being her normal self "Come on, guys, nothing can be that bad. Whatever it is you have to do today, just take a deep breath and Thank God that you're sitting there alive questioning some guy instead of laying somewhere in Sedona stone dead. Now order your food cuz I'm busy as all get out this morning."

They both sat there with a shocked, blank look on their faces and she suddenly spun away and said,

"Never mind, I'll think of something."

Ragetti and Smitty looked at each other and finally Ragetti grumbled "She's a damn mind reader too!" With barely time to gulp down their coffee, Donna was back with plates holding waffles, very crisp bacon and slices of bananas across their waffles to form a smiley face. She topped off their coffee, and was gone again.

Smitty looked at his plate of food and said, with a catch in his voice, "Damn I'm glad to be home again."

Ragetti reached out and patted him on the shoulder saying, "Me too, partner, me too!" As they reached the office they poked their head inside just long enough to let Patty know they would be in Brown's office. Smitty asked if there had been any calls.

Patty looked at the two of them and for the first time could see the strain on their faces. "Well there have been a couple of calls from the Interrogation Department wondering when you would be in. It appears Mr. Peters is raising quite the tantrum over there, telling them he's going to have them all fired and that's just for starters."

"If they call back, tell them to let him know if he keeps raising hell that they will be forced to put him in either Suicide or Solitary Confinement. We're on our way to Brown's office now."

As soon as they stepped inside Headquarters Deputy Director Brown had his door open and was beckoning them to come on in. "Have some coffee" he told them both. "I think we'll need it."

They both got coffee and settled down for a long talk. Ragetti started: "This was by far one of the worst assignments we've ever had. I may have to stop by and see the shrink." Brown gave him a sharp look, saw that he wasn't kidding; so said nothing.

Smitty said, "All the law enforcement in the entire area was very helpful. They are just not used to handling serious crimes up there.

So when we did get a few pieces of evidence, my partner drove them down to our Lab here and they gave it a priority standing, so with their results and Patty looking everything up on the computer, it helped a lot."

Ragetti interrupted with, "What he didn't tell you, Brown, is that he very nearly got his head blown off. If he hadn't at that second bent over to tie his shoe, I'd be needing a new partner and that's something I don't want to even think about. I fired at a shadow as it was about 2:00 a.m. and Sedona is not exactly lit up like the Vegas Strip. Sedona doesn't believe in street lights and probably most of the tourists don't care, but it's blacker than the Ace of Spades at night."

Brown threw up his hands. "Maybe it would be a good idea if we left out all the details on this assignment and just cut to the actual capture. The rest of it I can read in your reports. I can see that this has been a tough case on both of you, and I'm sorry."

Ragetti cleared his throat and continued, "We had DNA, tire tracks, everything including the address. I asked for the Sheriff and about seven other officers to go with us for the arrest. We didn't know what we might find in his house. Evidently when I took a shot at the shadow while checking out one of the famous landmarks at 2:00 a.m.; I evidently hit him because his leg was in a cast and that helped narrow things down too. Plus the pool of blood gave us his DNA.

Smitty stepped in with his observations, "With ten of us at his door the suspect did not give us any problem and he was alone in his house. The real shocker was when we entered his basement. It had a drive-in entrance from the back of the house, and it was set up like an operating room, plus in one corner was a large tub like structure with a lid. It contained muriatic acid. I don't know how you would test but the victims all went in there, so there isn't a trace. We have the names of those who were reported missing; but we don't know if that's all of them. The guy is crazy as a loon and evil. I think he's connected to some inner voice, alien, or whatever; or maybe it's just all in his crazy brain; but he was definitely following orders from someone."

Brown said, "I don't envy you having to face him and try to make sense out of an interview. The best thing to do is schedule him for a psychiatric evaluation. I doubt if he will be fit to stand trial, and he'll probably spend the balance of his life in a medical sanitarium."

"Well, we're on our way over to start the interview right now, he's been giving them a bad time, raising all kinds of hell, threatening to have them all fired, or worse."

As they entered the Interrogation Department three officers looked up with relief on their faces. "Holy Crap, are we glad to see you! What Interrogation Room do you want him in?"

Smitty, always the compassionate one, said, "I'm sorry you had to put up with him, just put him in Room One, and make sure he's handcuffed, and secure him also. I don't trust him as far as I can see him. You can handcuff his hands in front of him so he can drink water, and give him a bottle of water."

"I'd rather chain him to the wall," was the answer Smitty got. Soon he was secured in the room and reached for his bottle of water. From the way he was guzzling it down, the agents felt quite sure none had been offered to him.

Ragetti: "Tell me your full name and your most current address."

Peters: "My name is Richard E. Peters and my home is 1210 White Heron Dr. in Sedona, AZ 86336."

Ragetti: And how long has Sedona been your primary residence, Mr. Peters?"

Peters: "It's Dr. Peters to you, and I've lived there since 2013."

Ragetti: "Oh, I'm sorry, Dr. Peters, I didn't realize you were keeping your medical license up-to-date. And Dr. Peters, do you have any relatives in the immediate area, or do you live there alone?"

Peters: "I live alone, I moved to Sedona after my wife died. I have no children."

Smitty: "I'm sorry for your loss, Dr. Peters. Can you tell us a little about the activities of the various clubs you belong to in the vicinity of Sedona? It seems you are quite involved in several clubs, many of which lean toward believing in, or worshipping the occult and aliens from outer space. Could you tell us a little more about your beliefs?"

Peters: "I'm not the first person in the world to believe in aliens from outer space, and I will not be the last. Most people with any intelligence whatsoever; can see for themselves looking back over the past thousands of years, that Earth could not be where it is now without some outside help or interference. Aliens are so far ahead of us intellectually that it's like comparing the brain of a dog to his master. I myself have an IQ of 163 and when you read what the intellect of our world leaders are, it's obvious that the smarter you are, the more you are aware that you can't tell all the low-life on Earth about it or there would be chaos."

Ragetti: "So other than believing that there are aliens from outer space that have visited Earth, what else do you believe?"

Peters: "I not only believe that they have visited here, I believe they live here. They are scattered all over the world, taking on the shape of humans and gathering information until the time is right. Religious people speak of Armageddon or the End of the World; I doubt the aliens would use the same choice of words, but it could be construed as being in the same time frame."

Smitty: "So when this information-gathering is over and the aliens are ready for the showdown, will there be a big war, a fire, an explosion, a flood or what? And who will remain on Earth, if there is still an Earth that is inhabitable?"

Peters: "The aliens will survive minus several casualties I'm sure, and the humans who are on the side of the aliens will be changed over. The inhabitants of the Earth will not be as we think of aliens and will not be human. We will be a supreme race, far outreaching the goals of any one before us. We will be greater than those aliens of ancient times, who were still in the learning stages. Yes those ancient aliens could build astounding buildings and fly from one Planet to the next; but that is nothing compared to what they are capable of now."

Smitty: "If they are as advanced as you say, why do they seek to kill innocent human beings as I can see nothing gained from it?"

Peters: "Of course you can see no reason why anything would happen, but they are not killing humans for no reason, it is all part of the divine plan to give honor to the One Who Is Above All Others. He demands sacrifices and he lets us choose from the lower forms of humans to sacrifice rather than someone who is of significant importance. It is not because of compassion that they allow this; it is mainly to slowly decrease the number of undesirable humans. When the time comes all of the lower life humans will be eliminated before we are transformed into one Super Being."

Ragetti: "Did these aliens who are so much more intelligent than we are ever let you know how much time we have to accomplish this? Do we have a date with any proof or is it more like the idiots who predict a certain day as being the 'Last Day on Earth.' And then that sacred day comes and goes and everything is the same. What do you know for a fact?"

Peters: "Yes, for the average human you are very intelligent and very dubious to accept radical new knowledge. No, I have not been told a date, but I know it is coming soon, very soon. And there is nothing we can do to prepare ourselves or try to be one of the chosen few. It will either be or not be. I hope to be in favor with them for I have been very loyal to 'The One' by doing anything and everything he demands of me. You can't understand how it is to have a voice speaking to you inside your head – you can't get away from it. Even when I took a sleeping pill; I would go to sleep but I was besieged by endless dreams showing me what I must do and how I had to be very careful to never leave any clues."

Ragetti: "And to prove your loyalty you commit murder to comfort the mind of one who is evil enough to demand such morbid sacrifices?"

Peters: "From your point of view it would appear so, but your mind does not see the entire picture. Unless you have experienced what it's like to have a voice in your head telling you things you must do and how to do them, there is no way to understand how compelling it can be. Finally you can't think of anything except what the voice is telling you. And I think to try and explain it to you would be futile. Your mind is blocked to such new concepts. You and yours could very well make it through due to your desirable intelligence; but otherwise you will be lost forever. I can do nothing to help you."

Smitty: "But didn't you feel any remorse taking innocent people, people you didn't even know and just throwing them into that tub of acid?"

Peters: "The first time I did it, I felt bad for the young man; he had his entire life ahead of him. But I had given him an injection out on the trail so he would not put up a struggle. The only way I could fulfill the wishes of 'The One' was to destroy all evidence and leave no clues at all. And as a doctor I had gone over in my mind what is the best way to eliminate a body or parts of a body with no trace. There is always cremation but even then you are left with a small bag of bones that have not burned completely, and where would I hide them? And how would I explain to the electric company in Sedona how I was using so much electricity. I could have used gas I suppose, but I tried to eliminate any clues that would draw suspicion. Eventually I came up with the idea of the muriatic acid. The victims never suffered any pain at my hands at all; they were all heavily sedated before being placed in the tank."

Ragetti: "That's very compassionate of you. You didn't cause the victims to suffer any pain, but you still killed them. And if in the end only the most supreme being that will be left to inhabit Earth, who will do the menial jobs? The world will still need laborers and food."

Peters: "I didn't get into discussions to that depth as yet. I can't answer you."

Ragetti: "I think our interview is over."

Peters: "What are you going to do now?"

Ragetto: "Ordinarily an arraignment before the judge would be scheduled within the next day or two; but in your case, my boss wants a thorough psychological evaluation before you ever see the judge. That will be the next available appointment that is open, and you will be transported to the facility. I don't know exactly how long the evaluation will take, that will be totally up to them. Let me know if you need anything. You will be held in the holding area until we are notified that they are ready to do the psychological evaluation."

Ragetti and Smitty both stopped by Brown's office on their way back to write up their reports. Brown listened to their story with sympathy for he knew to rattle these two agents it had to be pretty bad. "He's completely off his rocker and believes that someday the more intelligent people on Earth will somehow be transformed along with the aliens to form a Super Being Race. I told him the next step will be a complete Psychological Evaluation, and that will take place at the very first available opening."

Brown: "I want you two to take a couple days off after the endless hours you've been putting in. And if you feel like checking in with our Shrink while you're off, go right ahead. I am all for it myself. So we'll check back with you in a couple of days."

Ragetti knew his wife was on the night shift which ended at 8:00 a.m., but he did want to talk to her about this before he jumped right into it. So he took a chance and called home. She picked up on the first ring. "Hi Sweetheart, I wondered if you had thirty minutes or so available so we could have a talk, but anytime you need to get some sleep, just let me know."

Victoria smiled to herself, "I always have thirty minutes for my favorite man; are you going to come home or am I meeting you?"

Ragetti told her he was coming home because Brown had just given Smitty two days off. "And he did the same thing for his partner, how about that? That's not even counting the weekend, so we really have four entire days off."

"I'd say you have a smart boss, see you in a few minutes, Handsome." And she hung up.

Ragetti pulled into the driveway, parked his car and went inside the house to see what his wife would think of his going to see a shrink. He had never gone willingly in his entire life. Victoria was sitting in the sitting room with two glasses of wine poured, and she told him he was welcome to take a nap with her when they finished their talk.

She thanked her lucky stars that he trusted her with his most inner thoughts and emotions. He sat down next to her, giving her a quick hug, then taking a gulp of the wine, he started to talk.

"When I went to Sedona I thought the whole case was some elaborate joke. Just the kind of thing the weirdos in Sedona would find humorous. But when Smitty almost got shot in the head I changed my mind on it being a joke. And you're right, you can't tell Susan. It was the first night we were there and just on a hunch I decided to dress all in black and go check out a place famous for hiking. Not that we intended to do any real hiking. I'll tell you when the sun goes down in Sedona it is absolutely black, I mean you can't even see across the road."

Victoria laid her head on Ragetti's shoulder and squeezed his hand.

"The stories we heard ranged anywhere from some crazy crossdresser who spends his days walking up and down Highway 89A, all the way to one woman's neighbors, who claim they are aliens inhabiting human bodies. They were twenty five years old or so, sisters, very tall, slim, and very blonde with practically crew cuts. They looked normal, but their actions and speech soon gave them away as weird. They had moved so we didn't get to meet them."

Ragetti took another big gulp of wine and continued, "When Smitty and I would stop at one of the local dining spots, we let it be known that we were journalists working for a magazine called 'Hear the Truth' and our names were Paul Dodson (me) and David Erickson (Smitty). We would ask if anyone had any unusual stories to tell about people they had encountered in Sedona or if they had seen anything strange. And filled with all those stories, we probably shouldn't have gone out that first night – out into all that black, so dense and thick you could barely see a foot in front of you, and that only with a small flashlight. We went to the Village of Oak Creek, parked in front of the hardware store and walked toward Courthouse Rock. I was nervous as hell, but I had to put on a good front or Smitty never would have followed me. He half-way believes in all this science fiction crap and I don't know what might have been running through his mind."

At this point Ragetti put his head in his hands and his shoulders trembled. Victoria hugged him and whispered soothing little nothings into his ear, until he finally reached for his wine and finished it off.

Victoria took a sip of hers and refilled his glass. She had never seen Ragetti like this, and it had her worried.

Ragetti said, "I'm OK, really – it's just at that same split second Smitty bend down to tie his shoe and we heard a bullet whiz over his head. I took a shot at a shadow about thirty feet in front of us and I thought I heard a cuss word followed by some crashing through the bushes along the path, and then absolute stillness. I didn't know if I had hit something or not, but with Smitty almost getting hit there was no *way we were going* to explore further. We were literally at the bottom of the rock; and we decided we'd come back early in the morning and see if there was any blood splatter.

We got up early the next morning, I mean like at five a.m. and I called the Park Rangers to close off that trailhead so we wouldn't lose any evidence."

Victoria looked shocked, "You mean Smitty narrowly escaped death and you aren't going to say a word about it to Susan? What if he tells her later and she thinks we withheld the information from her? Some friends we would be!"

"Victoria, I'm sorry, it's just how it has to be for now. I'm going to talk Smitty into seeing the shrink too, he's in bad shape. Spooked to the core, and rightly so, I hope we never go through anything like this again. Anyway, we went back and there was blood splatter and actually a pool of blood just off the trail. The man that shot at us is obviously familiar with the area and he took a different way down; but with the help of the Park Ranger we followed his trail and came to the spot he had parked his vehicle. Tire tracks of something big were evident. I took a picture, had a sample of the blood in an evidence bag – but they have no facilities in a tiny place like that. The worst thing that happens is a minor car crash or someone has their purse stolen. So I dropped Smitty off at the motel and told him to get some rest, and I drove down to our Lab here."

As Victoria gave him a hard punch in the arm, he looked at her,

"Baby, believe me, I was so eager to see you, touch you, I would not have been able to go back up to Sedona. I just got all the info that Patty had gathered up, got the results of the tire tracks and was back in the car on the way to see how my partner was doing.

Somehow Patty was able to dig through the records of the two different counties Sedona crosses and she came up with a make, model, owner's name and a Sedona address.

When I found Smitty talking as usual and drinking iced coffee, we took a ride up to the address – that's a story in itself. I'll tell you all about the house and the scenery as we eat dinner tonight. His house was at the end of a long winding drive, very private and very high dollar. We felt we were being watched from the minute we turned up his driveway. It had the address 1210 White Heron Drive posted on a sign and also the words 'Private Drive' although it did not say No Trespassing, it may as well have. I'm sure not many people would be confident enough to travel into the unknown."

"So you actually came face to face with this demon?" Victoria sputtered.

"I had Smitty stay in the car; I had a scrap of paper in my hand with the address written on it. When a man answered the door, I made up a name and asked if this was his residence. I felt like his eyes looked right into my brain and he knew every thought in my head. But worst of all is that he fit the description of the man a woman had told us a strange story about. Height, hair color, everything fit him to a tee. I knew in my heart he was the killer. He told me I had the right address, but no one by that name lived there. In fact, the name did not sound familiar for any of his neighbors either. He let me know he had the house built when he moved to Sedona, so it would never have been under a different owner."

"What did you do then?" Victoria asked.

"What anyone with any brains would do; got the hell out of there as fast as we could. We went directly from there to see the Sheriff to ask for backup and within an hour there were ten of us knocking on his door, guns drawn and search warrant in place. The night I shot at the shadow I had struck him in the leg, hence the large amount of blood. His leg was in a cast.

But the horrible part was the basement. It had a private drive-in from the back of the house, so he's been planning this ever since he moved to Sedona. His basement had a sterile operating room, and it is probably where he fixed up his own leg. But the sickening shocker was what he had done with the people who had come up missing. In one corner of the room was a very large, covered tub or vat filled with muriatic acid. He just dumped them in there, dead or alive, I don't know. The smell turned your stomach. The muriatic acid is bad enough, but when you add the smell of the bodies that had been dissolved in the acid the smell was horrible."

"OK, that's enough for now. And you are definitely going to see the Psychiatrist over this one – and so is Smitty. I know you said Brown gave you a couple of days off, but I think you will be seeing the doctor for quite some time. This is not only hard to take, it is just plain evil."

Ragetti said he was going to call Smitty and see if he had talked with Susan as yet. Once on the phone he could tell by his tone of voice that he had not said a word. "I just had a long talk with Victoria, and believe me, just getting it all out of my head and letting her know what we had been through has been a big help. I want you to sit down with Susan right now while you're alone and tell her about what's in your head. Sit next to her so she can touch you and call me back when you are done. Victoria wants to come over to see both of you after you have talked so I want you to get this done NOW! By the way, we are both going to make appointments with the Psychiatrist, and we're going to keep those appointments. I think this was even harder on you than me, but I was spooked and don't want to go through another experience like that real soon."

Smitty was going to object, say he was fine; but finally something just snapped and all the bravado just left his body and he told Ragetti he would talk to Susan right now.

"Honey, I've convinced Smitty to talk to Susan and if he needed us we could come over for an hour or two. I know you just got done working all night, and it will be a couple of hours or more before Smitty would be calling us, so why don't we take a nap. You need it."

"Sounds like a plan to me, before we do that are you hungry at all?"

"Nope, let's go – it is nap time for the bride and groom, and I do mean a serious nap."

Feeling very refreshed and so much better, Ragetti opened his eyes and saw Victoria was already up, and probably in the kitchen cooking something. He started down the stairs just as his cellphone rang and it was Smitty. "Do you feel a little better now?" was his question instead of saying hello.

Smitty laughed, and told him, "Yes, I do feel a lot better, and it's kind of funny because if anyone had told me ahead of time that all this stuff in Sedona would leave me needing a shrink I would have told them they were crazy. Hell, I half believe in aliens, not some of the weird stuff, but I just have a hard time describing what this trip did to me. Susan would like to see Victoria and if you want you can eat with us. I know Victoria worked graveyard last night -- so we'll eat and talk at the same time. Check with the Queen Bee and see if it's yah or nay."

By this time Ragetti was in the kitchen so he put his hand over the phone and told Victoria about Smitty's request. She looked around the kitchen at some half started food, but smiled and said 'let's go.' Ragetti told Smitty they were on the way, but they could only stay an hour or so. And they were on the way.

When they got to Smitty's house it seemed strangely quiet. Susan stuck her head out of the kitchen and laughed, "Welcome to the Morgue, we sent the boys to a movie so we could have a little peace and quiet. Hope you are both hungry, because I made chicken and dumplings. Soul food, so it's sure to help us all."

As they said a special prayer, with each person adding their thoughts, there was a feeling of calm and happiness settling over the table. Being with friends was good.

Smitty spoke up first to tell Ragetti he had already gotten an appointment with the shrink. And as long as I was at it I decided to make an appointment for you too. We are due in his office at one o'clock tomorrow. He may talk to us together and separately both. He won't know until we get in there.

"You outdid me, my friend. But good for you, I'm glad it's taken care of."

TWO WEEKS LATER

Brown received a phone call from the Psych Evaluation on Richard L. Peters to let him know what to expect. It didn't sound at all promising; but they were ninety-nine percent sure that Mr. Peters would not be standing trial. They had not yet figured out just what to call the things that went through his mind, but he was a danger to himself and others, so it would be extensive therapy and an even longer time period before they would even trust him around others.

Brown also put in a call to see how his two best agents were doing. The news on them was much better than what he heard about Peters. But the psychiatrist suggested "they stay off work this week and when they did come back, try to give them a case that doesn't sound like it's going to mess with their brains again. Personally, if I were them I'd never go back to work, but they have both indicated they need to have something to do."

"That sounds like my agents, they can't endure sitting around doing paperwork and not be on the job figuring out a crime and how to prove the guy is guilty," Brown responded. After those two phone calls, Brown sat at his desk and leaned back. He had never thought the case in Sedona would have such a traumatic effect on his two best agents. I would never forgive myself if they left the FBI over this, it was all my fault; I definitely owe them both. But the Psychologist said they were eager to come back to work, and their visits with him would still continue for quite some time.

Well, he mused, enough for random thoughts, it was time he made a call to both of them to see if they really wanted to come back to work. Did they think they were ready? Brown called Ragetti first. He picked up the phone on the second ring,

"Ragetti here."

"Hi Ragetti, this is Brown. Just wondered how you were feeling and see if maybe you had an estimate of when you might be ready to come back to work. And by the way our Psychiatrist has cleared both you and Smitty, but I want to hear it from both of you as to how you feel about returning to work."

"I'm glad to hear that, Brown. I guess you'll be calling Smitty next, so seeing tomorrow is Friday, why don't you plan on both of us coming back then, that way we can kind of ease into the work routine again."

Brown was smiling as he answered, "That sounds like the Ragetti I know. Damn! It will be good to have you both back. See you tomorrow."

Ragetti smiled too, and told him, "Yes, see you tomorrow, boss."

Ragetti turned to Victoria and told her "It looks like I won't be underfoot much longer as both Smitty and I are scheduled to return to work tomorrow.

Victoria smiled and said, "Good I knew it was coming soon. You've been moping around the house like you were being kept a prisoner."

"Oh, come on, I haven't been that bad, have I?" Ragetti retorted.

"Let's just say it will be good to see you return to normal again," Victoria said quietly.

So all three of them; Patty, Smitty, and Ragetti were back in the office Friday morning, all were wondering what sort of case Brown would come up with for them. They didn't have long to wonder, as Patty answered the phone it was Brown saying he wanted Ragetti and Smitty to report to his office. They lost no time in answering his command.

Brown looked the two agents over and saw by all appearances they looked quite normal. He took out a package from his desk and opened it. Inside were reports of kidnappings that had taken place in the Las Vegas area, and in the same package reports of females being raped and killed in the Kingman area. "The local police in Kingman have no jurisdiction to go to Las Vegas to question people, and to have several cases hit them at one time, they just don't know what to do. They need someone with authority to cross the state line and go freely from Arizona to Nevada. Police from the Nevada side could accompany you to the Arizona side as back-up for you and the same holds true of the Arizona Police in Kingman accompanying you to the Nevada side, being there as your back-up. Crossing the state line puts it in our jurisdiction, and it sounds like something you boys could sink your teeth into."

"So this is actually another out-of-town assignment for us," Smitty stated.

"Yes, it is out of town, but not so far that you can't come home every couple of days. Our lab is much better than they have in small towns, and the Kingman Police Department is anxious to have this case closed as soon as possible. I expect you two agents to head that way on Sunday afternoon so you will be there, ready to start working on Monday morning."

And so our Agents Ragetti and Smitty are off on their next assignment. Be sure to check our website to learn of this new adventure and how they solve it.